# Come Home My HEART

# Come Home My HEART

Phyllis Staton Campbell

Library of Congress Control Number:          2020912708

HARDBACK:              978-1-952155-61-1
PAPERBACK:             978-1-952155-60-4
EBOOK:                 978-1-952155-62-8

Ordering Information:

For orders and inquiries, please contact:
1-888-404-1388
www.goldtouchpress.com
book.orders@goldtouchpress.com

Printed in the United States of America

For Lydia, who kept the faith

Come Home, My Heart

# Chapter One

S usan sat beside the hospital window, trying to control the fear that seemed to bounce like a ball with every beat of her heart. In the driveway below, an ambulance moaned to a stop at the emergency entrance, just as the outside lights came on to turn the dusk into a semblance of day. Susan shivered as she fought against the thought that soon, her world would forever be like the approaching night.

Until that day, she couldn't remember ever having said so much as good morning to Dr. Ritchie. After all, her residency was in OB/GYN, and he was head of Neurosurgery. She had seen him, of course, as he made his way through the halls with a swarm of interns and residents following, but she had been too busy keeping up with her own swarm to give him much thought. Tomorrow he would hold not only her world but also her life in his hands.

"I'll have to be absolutely honest with you, Susan," he had said that afternoon, sitting on her bed while she occupied the armchair by the window. "I always try to be honest with my patients, but you're a doctor, and that puts even more of a burden of honesty on my shoulders. You'd know if I didn't tell you the truth. Like everybody else, you wouldn't want to face the truth, but you'd spot the lie."

"And the truth is?" She realized that she didn't want to know. She didn't want to be treated like a responsible adult. She wanted someone else to hear the truth; someone who would accept the pain and protect her the way adults protect children from the knowledge of death.

"I can save your life," he continued, his words seeming to echo her thought, "but I'm sorry, Susan, I can't save your sight. The tumor is benign, and at present, it poses no threat to your life, but we can't wait. The rate of growth seems to be rapid. The problem is that in order to remove it, I'll have to sever the optic nerve."

"What are you trying to tell me?" She was surprised to hear that her voice sounded almost normal.

"I think you know what I'm telling you. As much as I would like to do so, I can't save your sight. After the surgery, you'll be totally blind. I wish it could be different, but it can't, and the law, as well as my own conscience, says that you have to be told."

"Couldn't you be wrong, Dr. Ritchie?" "No." The single word had seemed as loud as a clap of thunder on a humid night, and there was no way to stop the storm from coming.

Now, as she sat watching the sky grow dark, she wondered if her life would be worth saving.

She could not remember when she had not wanted to be a doctor. While other little girls had been dressing their dolls and creating new hairstyles for them, she had been inventing and curing exotic diseases for hers. What her mother had called her surgery phase had followed when most of her doll patients were missing one or more parts. Then the playing stopped one rainy fall day when she was twelve. That was the day the cat had appeared on the front porch, a sodden gray ball of misery. It had refused to take no for an answer and was soon consuming unbelievable amounts of food in the kitchen.

"We'll name him Jasper," she had said, and although "he" later proved to be a "she", the name had stuck.

They really had intended to have Jasper "fixed," as her grandmother put it; but nature had fooled them all, and Jasper began to grow and grow. A box had been prepared for her in the garage, but Jasper --in the way of her kind--decided otherwise, choosing Susan's bed instead.

As Susan stood watching the almost unrecognizable creatures--four of them--make their way into the world, she knew what area of medicine would be her life's work. She had discovered the miracle of birth--the blood, the pain, and finally, the joy.

Over the years, she had never even considered changing her decision to become an obstetrician, and she had graduated at the top of her class. Her residency here at Clarington University had been easily won. Now it would all be over, all gone with one stroke of the surgeon's knife.

And then she thought of Eric. How on earth could she tell him that it would all have to end?

They had met at a party given by one of the other medical students. Although she wouldn't go so far as to say that it had been love at first sight, neither had dated anybody else.

Eric had a degree in business administration, and he worked in a small but prestigious advertising firm.

"I'll be one of the partners by the time I'm thirty," he had told her the night he had asked her to marry him. "There won't be any penny-watching for us."

"I can't give up my work, Eric, not even for you, for us," she'd answered, and she had moved a little away from him, but not out of his arms.

"Of course not. I'm not that out of date. We'll rake in the money between us. A society practice for you, with someone junior to do the dirty work, such as calls in the middle of the night. We'll be the darlings of society, wait and see."

In anger now, she tried to stop the tears. She never cried, not even when both her parents had died in a plane crash during her first year in med school. Using the time tears would have taken, she had found an evening job typing medical records to replace the allowance they had been giving her and had gone on with her work. Only now, there could be no work, no going on.

With an angry jerk, she pulled a handful of the flimsy hospital tissues from the box on the table next to her chair and dabbed at her eyes.

"You'd better pull yourself together," she said aloud, "because he'll soon be here."

Every evening since she had been admitted to the hospital for tests to find the cause of her repeated headaches and dizziness, Eric had stopped by after work, staying with her against her protests until eight-thirty, when the public-address system ordered all visitors to leave.

Feeling that she would soon wake and find this whole day was only a bad dream, she went to the small bathroom and put on fresh makeup.

Eric's familiar double knock sounded just as she finished.

"Come in," she called, amazed to hear that her voice sounded the way it always did.

"You're looking bright and lovely," he said, holding her away from him after he had kissed her. "When will you be able to go home? Old man Lewis from Tasty Pet Products is coming next week and bringing his fat wife along. I'll need a hostess. It'll be a bore for both of us, but if I land that account, we'll take about six giant steps up that good old ladder."

"Eric, I--" And to her horror, she began to cry, not just tears, but big, long sobs that wouldn't stop.

"Oh, darling, did I say something?" he asked, dropping to his knees. "I was just kidding. The Lewises are okay. I wanted to make you laugh. Hey, just think about the promotion I'll get when you and I land that account. Stop crying."

But she couldn't stop, and in the end, the nurse had come and given her an injection.

"She'll be all right," she told Eric. "Tears are common the evening before surgery."

"Surgery!" And the nurse actually backed away, realizing too late what she had done. "What do you mean? She's just here for tests. Don't you even know what your patients are doing in the hospital?"

"Sir, I--"

"It's all right, nurse." For the life of her, Susan couldn't remember the woman's name. "I'll take care of it. You made a mistake but learn from it. Now please go, and close the door."

"Now, what's all that about?" Eric took both her hands.

"They finished the tests today, and it isn't good, Eric. There's a tumor--No, don't look like that. It's operable. But, oh, darling, if only I didn't have to tell you. ..."

"You don't have to tell me anything. All I care about is that you'll be all right, and you say they can operate. You will be all right?"

"If you mean, will I live--yes. But there's ... something else." She forced herself to breathe slowly and went on. "The tumor is very close to the optic nerve. In order to remove it, Dr. Ritchie will have to destroy the optic nerve. Eric, after tomorrow I'll be totally blind."

For long, agonizing minutes, he just sat there; then he took her in his arms, held her close, and stroked the auburn cloud that was her hair.

"It's all right," he said over and over. "I love you, and it's all right."

"But can't you see, Eric? This changes everything. My career, our marriage--everything's over, everything!"

"Nothing important is over, because you will go on being you. I can take this, but not losing you. What kind of person would I be to walk away from you and our plans now? Sure, you'll have to give up your plans for a career in medicine, and that's rotten luck. But we're still on, loud and clear, and don't you forget it."

"But--"

"Look, we made an agreement, and I for one, am going to stick to it. Now, you just work on getting well."

# Chapter Two

For the next five days, Susan rested in the comfort of the womb that was hospital routine. Her every need was provided by willing and sympathetic hands, but on the sixth day, things began to change. She suddenly realized that whether she liked it or not, she would have to come to terms with her new world.

"Have you made plans for when you'll leave the hospital?" Once again, Dr. Ritchie sat on her bed while she sat beside the window, with the view she could no longer see.

"What do you mean?" she asked. "What's to plan?"

"Susan, you have to face it. Your life can't go on just as before. In a way, you'll be entering a whole new world. You'll find that you'll have to relearn the simplest things, and that's just the beginning."

"How can I do anything?" The statement surprised her, but he seemed to expect it.

"This isn't the time to discuss that, Susan. You know deep inside yourself that there are a lot of things you can do, and of course, there will be things you'll never be able to do again. The thing now is to decide what your first step will be. You're ready to leave the hospital, speaking from a medical standpoint. Where will you go?"

"I hadn't thought about it," she admitted, knowing in spite of her self-pity that he was right. "Back to my apartment, I suppose."

"Do you live alone?"

"Yes. It's a small place, and I guess I sort of like my own company. I'm an only child, and to tell the truth, I've never quite been able to enjoy someone else around all the time."

"I can understand that," he said, "but you may find that you'll need somebody for a few days. Is there anyone--your mother, an aunt--anyone who could stay with you for a while, or maybe someone you can go to? I would rather you went back to your apartment if you mean to go on living there, but if that's impossible, we'll just have to work around it."

"There's no one. Oh, there are a few cousins, but I hardly know them."

"All right, then, we'll just have to go with the situation as it stands. I'm going to contact the Department for the Visually Handicapped. They'll help you get started with sorting out your personal life, and later you'll be able to start thinking about employment. Okay?"

"No, not okay. I'm perfectly capable of taking charge of my own life. If you think for one minute I'm going to have somebody tell me how to live, you're mistaken. I've always taken care of myself--well, at least, for the last few years--and I'm not going to stop now."

"Susan," the doctor said, crossing to lay his hand on her shoulder, "no one is going to try to tell you how to live your life, but we all need help at one time or another. Look at it from this angle: Suppose you had a patient, let's say a very young patient, who suddenly found herself the mother of triplets. This young woman knows absolutely nothing about babies, and here she is with three of them. She has no mother, no one to advise her. Wouldn't you say she needs help, and wouldn't you try to help her get it?"

"Well, yes, of course, but that's a different matter."

"Why?" She heard him go back and sit down. "It isn't the same." She could feel the blood rush to her face, a sure sign that she was beginning to get angry. "For one thing, she wouldn't be acting for herself alone; there would be the babies to think about."

"Okay, I'll give you that, but you have others to consider too. What about that guy who's been so concerned about you? Don't you think you owe him something? I think you do, but even more than that, you owe yourself a lot. Now, I have to get to the office. I'm going to send you home the day after tomorrow, so think about what we've discussed."

And she did think, all through the long night, and part of the next day.

They had just taken away her untouched lunch tray when a knock sounded at her partially open door.

"Come in," she said, not even wondering who it was. She just didn't care that much.

"Dr. Perry?" said a firm yet feminine-sounding voice.

"Yes?" Not more lab work! She thought.

"I'm Anne Davenport from the Department for the Visually Handicapped. I know I should have called first, but I had another appointment in this part of town and finished before I expected to. May I come in?"

"I think you're already in." She knew it sounded rude, but she didn't care.

"Yes, but I'll go away if you really want me to. I just came by to get acquainted, but if it's not a good time--"

"No, I guess this is as good as any. Did Dr. Ritchie call you?"

"Not personally, but he made a referral yesterday and asked if someone could drop by before you go home tomorrow. You know that state law requires him to report cases to us, and requires that we make at least one effort to see if we can be of any help."

"Well, you've both done your duty, so go." She knew she was going to cry. How she hated the tears that seemed so ready to come to the surface! How she hated her weakness! How she hated herself.

"I hate myself," she surprised herself by saying, not in her thoughts, but out loud.

"I know. So do I still, sometimes. All right if I sit on the bed?"

"I guess so. Oh, I'm sorry--sit down, of course. I'm not usually this rude. I don't know what's wrong with me."

"You're blind," her visitor said, and Susan could hear her settling herself on the bed. "That's enough to make a person rude and a lot of other things. Overnight, your whole world has tumbled and left you nothing to take its place--at least, nothing that you can see right now."

"See--that's funny. I can't see anything --not with my eyes or with my mind or with my heart. It's all gone, my life as I've always known it; my work, everything."

"It seems like that. I know."

"How can you possibly know?" Her voice seemed to raise an octave with the anger inside her. "You were free to cross streets, find the elevator, and come to my room. You're free to go home at the end of the day. Your life belongs to you."

"You're right, Susan. I did come here by myself and will leave here, go to the bus stop and from there to the office. This evening I'll cook dinner for my husband and children. I do understand, though, because I can't see, either. I lost my sight in an accident ten years ago, and I'll tell you a secret. My life seemed so futile at first that I actually wanted to end it. I even thought about ways to do it, but I went on one day after the other until things began to have meaning. You'll do the same thing. I'm not promising you that it'll be easy. It won't, but you'll make it."

"You're blind, totally blind?" The words came in a near whisper.

"Yes."

"You really can do all those things? Traveling and cooking?"

"Cross my gizzard," Anne said in a sudden rush of humor, which Susan was to learn often covered stronger emotion. "It took some doing. I should have been given a prize for the clumsiest being the agency ever trained, but they reserved the honor, hoping for someone else. Of course, you'll be able to do all those things. It'll take a lot of hard work and more patience than you can imagine, but I promise, you can."

"But--"

"Listen, Susan--it's okay if I call you Susan, isn't it?"

Susan nodded, and then realized what she had done; Anne wouldn't have seen her. "You can call me anything you want to," she said, "if you'll just help me find my way around this new world of mine. Dr. Ritchie told me it would be like a new world."

"He's right too," Anne told her, "although I expect that even he doesn't know just how new it is. It takes one to know one--Well, you know what I mean. I know something of what you're feeling because I've been there. I can't know exactly what you're feeling, because we're all different."

"I think what worries me the most is my work," Susan said. "There's no way I can go on with it, but it's my whole life."

"Now, that's one of those differences I was talking about. I was a senior in high school. One of those uncertain kids of the seventies who had no idea what to do with their lives. When I lost my sight, I wanted to die, as I told you. Then one morning, I woke up to the fact that life does have a purpose. I still didn't know just what it was for me, but I just went on from there. I can see how much harder it has to be for you. You'll have to reshape your career plans rather than find them in the first place."

"Didn't you find it hard to marry and have a family?" Susan asked, feeling rather as though she was prying, but Anne didn't seem to mind.

"No, but we met in my senior year at the university. I'd come to terms with my blindness by then. You're engaged, Dr. Ritchie told me. How do you feel about it? Or rather, maybe more to the point, how does he feel?"

"He's been fantastic. He's in advertising, and we had so many plans. He says that nothing's changed. He keeps telling me he'd never walk out on me now."

"He hasn't voiced any doubts at all?" Anne asked.

"None at all," Susan said. "He just keeps telling me that he'll never walk out on me and how nothing has changed."

Anne sat without speaking for a moment; then Susan heard her get off the bed.

"Okay, kid. I've got another appointment in fifteen minutes, and I've already missed my bus. I'll grab a cab, but I've got to get going. Dr. Ritchie says you're going home tomorrow."

"That's right. Anne, I--I'm afraid. I don't know if I can manage."

"I know. Look, how are you going to get there, and will anyone be there with you?"

"I don't know." You're not going to cry, not again, she told herself. "I suppose Eric would pick me up. There's nobody--"

"Okay, hang tough. This is what we'll do. I'll call Dr. Ritchie when I get back to the office and find out just what time he's going to release you. Someone from the office with a car and I will pick you up. I'll try to get Judy; she's the gal who'll be teaching you to get from point A to point B as soon as you're ready. She can get started by teaching--or rather re-teaching--you how to get around in your apartment. We'll arrange for Meals on Wheels for you, at least for a week or two. Does this sound all right, or would you rather do something else? I want you to feel good about things. I'm not here to be a parental figure, so tell me if I'm out of line."

Susan tried to answer around the lump in her throat. She had known, of course, that Eric would be there for her; he had told her so--but she had felt so alone. Now, at least for a little while, someone who knew, someone who understood, would help her over the rough places.

"All right?" Anne asked softly.

"Sure," she said.

"Okay, see you tomorrow. I'll call you, though, and tell you exactly what time."

As she left the room, Anne's steps sounded brisk and confident, and for the first time in a week, Susan felt her own confidence start to grow again.

# Chapter Three

Susan had expected her mood of confidence to lessen through the long afternoon, but to her surprise, it didn't.

She wished that she knew what time it was. There were so many little things that bothered her. Of course, here in the hospital, there were sounds, all so familiar to her, that gave her an idea of the time: the sound of the linen cart in the morning; the voices of the new shift of nurses and orderlies; and, of course, the smell of food as the trays were wheeled along the hall at mealtime. It wasn't the same, though. She missed being able to look at her watch and to know just what time it was.

Now the smell of green peppers told her that her dinner would soon be served, and that meant Eric would soon be there. In fact, if dinner wasn't early, he was later than usual, and she realized that this wasn't the first time in the past few days that he had come late.

"Well, really!" she scolded herself. "You're getting like a petulant old lady, counting the seconds. He could have been delayed in traffic, or a dozen other things."

"Talking to yourself, doctor?" the aide said as she put her tray on the table. "I hear that's a bad sign."

"Worse than bad, Olive," she said, absurdly glad she could recognize the girl's voice. "I'll be answering myself next."

"Well, just see you say the right thing. The nurse will be here in a minute to help you find things. See you."

"Right."

When, she wondered, would she be able to say "see" as casually as Anne had done? Soon, she told herself, but this time she didn't speak aloud. That was another thing she found hard. You never knew when someone was watching you.

She had just finished her ice cream when Eric came. To her delight, she recognized his step from down the hall.

"Hi," he said and bent to kiss her cheek. "Is that the best you can do?" she asked, turning her face up for a real kiss.

"Well, yes, with half the hospital watching."

"Hardly half the hospital, and why should we care?"

"You sound chipper tonight. What's up?" And he moved a chair so he could take her hand.

"Oh, I don't know," she said. "No, that's not true. I had a visit today from Anne Davenport from the Department for the Visually Handicapped. Eric, for the first time I--well, I'm beginning to hope."

"Hope what?" He gave her hand a little squeeze and laid it on her lap.

"Oh, I don't know any particular what, just hope. She's been blind for ten years, and you wouldn't believe the things she does. She has a home and children, and--"

"Hey, not so fast! We're not even married," he interjected, and she could imagine his smile as he spoke.

15

"Oh, Eric! You know what I mean. Her life is"--she searched for the right word-- "normal."

"Well?"

"I'm going to ignore you." But for some reason, she felt disappointed. Meeting Anne had meant so much to her; all afternoon she had thought about telling him, and now, he didn't even seem to want to listen.

"She called late this afternoon to tell me that she and the O-and-M instructor from her office will pick me up and drive me home tomorrow afternoon."

"What on earth is an O-and-M instructor? She sounds dangerous."

"Oh, Eric, can't you be serious?" She made it sound as though she was teasing, but part of her meant it. What was wrong with him?

"Well, what is it? Or should I say, who is she, or what is she?"

"She's the Orientation-and-Mobility instructor. Anne says she'll start by teaching me how to get around in the apartment."

"Look, babe, you don't need all that.

You'll know how to get around in your own apartment. You've lived there for three years. Don't let them make you believe that you can't. Oh, I know they mean well. After all, they do help a lot of people and do a great job. But you're different. After all, you belong to me."

"Please be serious, Eric. That has nothing to do with it. Can't you understand?"

"Of course I understand. I don't want you worrying about it, that's all. A lot of times these things work out all by themselves. Go along with your what's-it instructor if it'll make you feel better."

For a long time that night, Susan lay awake, thinking. She knew Eric loved her, and that he only wanted what was best for her. The question was what was best for her? If only someone could understand how confused she was. If only someone could tell her what to do with herself, with her life.

But that's simple, she told herself. You're going to marry Eric and do all the things you've planned.

"Remember, you're still my Susan," he had said when he had kissed her good night. "Nothing has changed."

If only she could believe that! But something deep inside her kept telling her that things had changed. Could they go on with all their plans?

She reasoned that the inner part of her--the part that loved and laughed and cried and lived--was just the same. Still, physically she was different, and the professional part of her, at least, knew that this physical change was real. She knew that she could not avoid that change, no matter how much she wanted to. As she fell asleep, she wondered if she could face her changed life alone, after all, and she wondered why she didn't remind herself that she had Eric.

"Here we are," Judy said, and Susan felt the familiar bump of the car against the curb. "Sorry about that," Judy said.

"I always do--did that. I don't know why, but almost everyone misjudges the distance here at my parking space," Susan said.

"Is the Nova in the other space yours?" Judy asked, and Susan heard the click of her seat belt as she started to get out of the car.

"Yes," Susan said. She felt a pang, knowing that she would never drive the little green car again.

"Did you get good mileage?" Judy asked as she opened Susan's door for her. "You can step right on the sidewalk; I'm against the curb, but you know that."

She had shown Susan how to walk, holding to her arm before they left the hospital, and now she touched Susan lightly with her elbow so that she knew where she was.

"We'll leave Anne to follow along behind. Okay, Annie?"

"That's the story of my life--always tagging along in the rear." And Anne closed the back door. "Sure, you guys trot right along, I'm fine."

"You have a nice, broad walk right up to the front door," Judy said, starting to walk along at a normal speed. "Careful back there, Anne--there's a limb sticking out a little. Oh, it's okay, you just passed it. Nasty things for cane travelers, limbs. There's no way to detect them. You have your key, I hope. We're at the door."

Feeling both awkward and a bit foolish, Susan felt around in her brown leather bag until she felt her ring of keys.

"I hope I can find the right one," she said. Now she really did feel foolish. They'd think she was stupid, and she wished she'd kept quiet.

"Try," Anne said, "and if you can't identify it, Judy's elected to find it by the tried-and-tested method of elimination."

"Gee, thanks," Judy said wryly. "I always get to have all the fun. Bet she's found the right one, though. It looks right."

In her mind, Susan saw the door and the dead-bolt lock. Very carefully, she felt and could have cried when she found the keyhole. She inserted the key and turned it to the right. There was a satisfying click. She turned the knob, and the door opened.

"Good girl." Judy gave her a little hug, and they went in.

"Oh, how attractive! Anne, it's done all in greens and golds. That sounds sort of icky, but it isn't. I wish it was easier to describe the different shades, but it's hard to do even for those of you who have been able to see. It's almost impossible to describe for those who have never been able to see."

"I hadn't thought about that," Susan admitted, "but how would they know what colors are like?" For the first time since she had lost her sight, she found something to be grateful for.

"They've missed a lot, haven't they? I mean, never to have seen, say, a sunset, or the color of the leaves in fall."

"Speaking of leaves," Judy said, "the leaves on the tree along your walk are starting to get green. Do they usually show this early? Isn't the end of March early?"

"Yes, but maybe they're welcoming me home." And she realized that it did feel and smell like home, and she felt a small joy at the knowledge.

That was a busy afternoon. Patiently and thoroughly, Judy reacquainted her with all the familiar things she had taken so for granted. Together, they rearranged things in the kitchen so that they would be easier for her to find. To her surprise, she found it easier than she had thought it would be to remember what colors her clothes were, and which looked best together. The sets of sheets and towels were a real problem until Judy folded them together.

"You may forget what color it is, but at least you won't put out a red towel and a pink washcloth. Later, when Anne teaches you Braille, you can get little metal color tags to sew in the corners, but this will hold you until then."

"How many things I've always taken for granted!" Susan said, sitting on the edge of the bed, which she and Anne had just finished making up with clean sheets--lavender, Judy had told them.

"You'll be finding new ones every day," Anne assured her. "Now come on, you're going to learn to make coffee. Instant or perk?"

"Well, usually instant except when I have company."

"All right, instant today, and perk next time." If anyone had told her that she would feel so much pride in making a cup of instant coffee, she would not have believed them. With that one simple accomplishment, she seemed to find faith in herself and in the shadowy future. She had been terrified of the hissing boiling water, but Anne showed her how to lift and pour safely, "over the sink for now." And before she knew it, all three of them were sitting at the kitchen table, sipping coffee.

"I have one more thing for you to master before we go," Anne told her when they had finished their coffee and Susan had washed the cups and put them in their place in the cabinet over the sink.

"Not something else!" she pretended to wail. "Oh, you'll like this," Judy told her. "It's sort of like a prize for work well done, isn't it, Anne?"

"Listen," Anne said.

"Three forty-five p.m.," a male voice said.

"What on earth!"

"Your prize." And Anne placed a small box in her hand. "It's a talking clock. You just press this button when you want to know the time. You can set it to tell the time every half hour, and it can be set like an alarm clock. We won't bother you with how to set it this time, but that'll be another of our lessons. If you want the alarm set, though, I'll do it for you before we go."

"Oh, no. This is wonderful." And she pushed the button again, just for the miracle of hearing, knowing, what time it was.

"Okay, then, hon, we're off," Anne said. "I'll call you tomorrow. Oh, yeah, I forgot the telephone. Can you preset numbers on your phone? If you can't, there's one with auto-dial in the car."

"I got one for Christmas, thanks. But you might go over the settings with me, please, Judy. And could you set a button for your office, Anne, just in case I--I mean--"

"Of course, it'll be all right for you to call if you have a problem," Anne assured her. "If I'm not there, ask for Judy. And if Judy is out, just tell the secretary what you need. Someone will help. Don't hesitate; that's what we're there for."

When she heard the sound of the car disappear down the street ten minutes later, Susan sank onto the sofa. It had been quite a day! She wondered if she could ever remember everything she had learned today, much less all the things they had promised she would learn later. Anne had explained that usually, new clients weren't given quite so many lessons in the first session, but they had tried to give her all she would need for living alone. They couldn't just leave her and hope she would find someone to help. Yes, it had been quite a day.

"Well," she said aloud to the little clock, "I've started. I don't know whether I'll ever get to that destination called independence, but I'm sure going to try." And as though in answer, the clock announced: "The time is four p.m."

# Chapter Four

T he rest of the afternoon seemed endless. Susan had never had so much time on her hands. She smiled, thinking how often she had wished for time.

Now that you have it, what are you going to do with it? She asked herself.

The telephone sounded its electronic chime. "You'll learn to hurry slowly," Anne had told her. And now, as she crossed the room in answer to the repeated rings, she realized just what Anne had meant.

"Hello, this is Susan Perry."

"Hi, Susan Perry. This is Eric Graham."

"Hi there. Would you like to speak to my clock?"

"Would I what? Susan, what are you talking about?"

"It's five-fifteen p.m.," the robot-like voice announced as she pushed the button.

"I'll admit his vocabulary is somewhat limited but isn't he wonderful?"

There was silence for what seemed an eternity, then Eric said, "Yeah, sure."

"Is that all you have to say?"

She knew that she was silly to expect the clock to mean as much to him as it did to her. Still, it did seem that he could have been glad just because she was.

"What do you expect?" he said lightly, and she sensed that his humor was strained. "I call my girl, and there's another man there. Look, how about dinner--or is your clock taking you out?"

"Out! Oh, Eric, I--I, yes, I'd love it."

"Okay, see you in about forty-five minutes." She was filled with fear and joy as she replaced the receiver. Dr. Ritchie had told her that it would be all right for her to go out, as long as she was careful not to go too far or get too tired. Well, out to dinner would hardly fit into either of those categories. It would be good to get out.

She had planned to have the sandwich and fruit Judy had bought for her on the way home, but this was great. Not only would a good dinner be welcome after the routine of hospital food, but she felt really good that Eric wanted to take her.

It was foolish, she knew now, but she had felt that he was uncomfortable with her. Oh, he had acted the same--well, almost the same--there was something different in his manner.

"Why wouldn't he feel a bit uncomfortable?" she asked herself. "He's probably afraid he'll do or say something wrong."

Olive at the hospital was right--she would have to watch talking to herself. Then she really did hurry, not quite so slowly this time, to the bedroom.

She would have time for a shower. Since her hair had been shaved for the surgery, one of the volunteers at the hospital had gotten her a wig and helped her style it the way she had always worn her hair. That meant she wouldn't have to worry about how her hair looked.

"Avoid the use of a lot of makeup until we can get around to that lesson," Anne had told her as they had arranged the bottles and jars on her dressing table.

"I don't wear much anyhow," she had said, sniffing a jar. There was no mistaking the scent of her cleanser, and she put it in the spot they had decided would be the right one for it.

"You should be all right then. Just remember that none looks better than to have it done all wrong. I still can't master nail polish, and to tell the truth, I don't know a totally blind woman who can. Maybe you'll be the exception."

"Hardly," she had said, placing a bottle of hand lotion in its position on the back row. "My work dictates short, scrubbed nails." Once again, she had felt the sense of sadness and loss she experienced whenever she thought about her work.

But now, standing in front of her closet, she did not feel sad. Her whole body tingled after her shower, and her heart was almost light as she moved her clothes along the rod.

Eric hadn't said where they were going, so she finally decided on her navy pantsuit and a frilly blouse to give it a dressy touch.

Remembering Anne's warning about makeup, she carefully applied a light foundation and just a touch of powder. She hesitated over lipstick; then, remembering the mornings she had put on her makeup while looking over her notes just before a test, she took the top off the tube and traced the line of her mouth. A drop or two of the perfume Eric had given her for her birthday, and she was ready.

The apartment was quiet except for the faint hum of the refrigerator and a gurgle in the pipes as the tenant above her ran water. Outside, a wind had risen, and rain hissed against the windows.

Eric was late, and again she reminded herself to stop counting seconds and minutes. Had she always done that, or was it what she thought of as a symptom of her blindness? She would have to watch that for her own sake as well as Eric's.

Of course, she knew that time meant more to her than it did to him. For the first time in her life, she was forced to sit and wait for the pleasure of others.

If she only had something to do, something with some meaning. Anne had mentioned employment, but that seemed as far away as had her childhood dreams.

A car door clicked, and she forced her thoughts back to the present. She was absurdly excited about the first dinner with Eric--excited and afraid all at the same time. Suppose she spilled something. Suppose there was nothing on the menu that would be easy for a blind person to handle. Oh, suppose a dozen things! But she reminded herself that Eric had faith in her ability, and she went to open the door.

She knew at once that it wasn't Eric standing there. It wasn't only the dainty, feminine smell of violets, but it just didn't feel like Eric. Eric was around six feet tall, and the person who stood there wasn't as tall as her own five-three. She had heard about so-called facial vision, which detects an object or person in front of the face; but for now, she just knew it wasn't Eric.

"Yes?" she said uncertainly. Probably it was someone selling something.

"Why, Susan dear, you're up and around! How nice."

Oh, no! She knew that she was expected to know the woman, but for the life of her, she couldn't recognize the voice.

Stalling for time, she said, "Yes, I got home from the hospital this afternoon."

Southern accent, under five-three, violet-scented perfume. How do you go about telling a person you don't know who she is? Well, she'd have to do something. They couldn't go on just standing there. Then--oh, blessed relief!--she heard Eric's step coming up the walk.

"Mother, what on earth are you doing, keeping Susan standing here practically in the rain? You'll both catch a cold."

"Well, darling, she hasn't asked me in yet. Of course, I'm sure she was about to do so, weren't you, Susan?"

"Yes, do come in," Susan managed to say, and then stood there feeling like an idiot, until Eric took her arm and guided her over to the sofa.

Now she recognized the voice, even that sickly sweet perfume. Penelope Graham --really, could she have been christened Penelope?-- straight from South Carolina, and not about to let the backwoods Virginians forget it. Not a kind thing to be thinking, Susan reflected, but who's responsible for her thoughts, anyhow?

"Did you get everything, son?" Penelope said, and Susan could hear her opening the coat closet. "Oh, Susan honey, there don't seem to be any empty hangers. I'll just pop into the bedroom and get some."

She heard Eric going to the kitchen, and then the rustle of bags as he put something on the counter.

"There, now." Penelope closed the closet with a little bang. "That door doesn't slide very well, dear. You'd better see about it."

Susan had a wild desire to tell her that she couldn't see but controlled herself just in time.

"Weren't you surprised to find Mother at the door?" Eric said, sitting on the other end of the sofa.

"I certainly was."

"You see, darling, I told you I should come." Now Penelope was rattling a bag.

"I'll just get my apron on, and we'll be eating in no time. I hope you like spareribs, Susan; Eric just adores them. I have the most marvelous recipe, and when Eric told me this morning he was coming over tonight to take you to dinner, I decided to surprise you both. Now you won't have to go out among a lot of people who might not understand-- Well, who might not understand about you."

All the time Penelope was talking, she was opening cabinets and setting things on the counter--from the bags, Susan hoped. She cringed as she heard dishes, pots, and pans rattled. What was happening to her careful arrangement? What had happened to the quiet, romantic dinner she had envisioned?

"I've already done most of the cooking at home.

Oh, dear! Where's your microwave?"

At last, Susan found her voice. "I don't have one."

"Oh, my goodness, honey, however do you manage? I couldn't cook a blessed meal without my little microwave. Oh, well, we'll manage. Now, Eric, you come and set the table. Where's your tablecloth? Oh, here it is."

Susan heard a drawer slide shut, and she wondered where Penelope had found that tablecloth. Susan hadn't seen it for ages.

"Isn't Mother something?" Eric said. "Yes, she certainly is." But Susan found herself wondering exactly what. She was good at finding tablecloths.

"Not like that, darling." Susan could hear Penelope rearranging something on the table in the dining alcove. "You'll have to learn a lot of things to help Susan. You'll both have to remember that things have changed. Now, dear, give me your little hand, and I'll just take you right over to your chair. There. Oh, don't you look sweet! Really, dear, almost no makeup is becoming."

Susan had found herself being gently pulled from the sofa and led across the room.

"Now, just help yourselves. I made a lot. Eric, darling, go get Susan another napkin."

"No, really. ..." To Susan's horror, she felt the napkin being tucked in at the neck of her blouse like a bib.

"Now, you're all fixed."

Susan knew that if she lived to be the oldest person on record, she would never forget the next thirty minutes or so.

First, there was the salad. How on earth was she going to manage tomato wedges and all that lettuce, drowned in dressing, sitting on a small flat plate?

"Why, Susan dear, you've hardly touched your salad," Penelope said.

"I guess I'm saving room for the ribs." What a mistake saying that turned out to be!

"Well, what a wise girl you are. I'll just take your salad, then, and bring in the main course. Darling, you really need a tea cart. We'll have to do some shopping. You'll have a lot of entertaining to do. It'll be a big responsibility, but don't worry, I'll advise you. It can't be easy for you."

"Mother, don't you think--"

Susan had been wondering if Eric had been struck dumb or something. He'd hardly spoken the whole evening.

"Oh, Susan doesn't mind me, do you, darling? We're all family. Now, Susan here's your plate."

As she explored with her fork, Susan realized that her worst fears were a reality. Her plate was loaded with whole ribs, a slippery sort of vegetable she was never able to identify, green peas, and of course, the barbecue sauce, which seemed to be going all over everything on the plate.

Now's when I find out whether there's a guardian angel for the blind, she thought as she picked up her knife.

To her amazement, she managed to cut a piece of meat and transport it safely to her mouth. One piece after another, she managed to eat, while Penelope babbled on about nothing.

Later she realized that overconfidence had been her undoing, or maybe she never had been doing as well as she thought. Whatever the reason, her knife suddenly slipped and the rib she was attacking went flying, picking up the sauce and some of the unidentified vegetables as it went. Off her plate they went, knocking against her cup of coffee; with a little plop the whole mess, including the coffee, landed in Penelope's lap.

One thing for sure, something had finally made the woman stop talking--right in the middle of a sentence lamenting the "deplorable number of foreigners who've moved--" Susan would never know where.

"Oh, Eric!" Penelope shrieked. "Get Mother a towel! Oh, my best dress! Now, it's all right, my dear, don't you worry a thing about it. Oh, dear! I know it'll never come out! Now, it's not a thing to worry about, Susan. These little things happen when we can't see. Well, Eric, don't just stand there, bring me a damp towel! What good do you think this one is?"

Susan began to tremble. She was never to know how much of her shakiness was physical weakness, how much was embarrassment at the accident, and how much was the effort to keep from crying and laughing all at the same time. In any case, she couldn't help herself, the remark just came out:

"Oh, Penelope, my dear, you should have had a bib like mine."

"Sorry we have to leave so early," Eric said ten minutes later, "but we'll have to try and clean Mother's dress."

"Sure, I understand."

"Darling, are you sure you don't want me to do the dishes?" Penelope asked fretfully. "Really, Eric's making too much of a fuss about this. I'm afraid washing up will be too much for you--all that grease, I mean. Are you sure you'll be able to get things clean? Dirty dishes can spread germs, you know."

"Yes, I know, but I can manage," Susan assured her. "I really think cold water will take care of your dress until you can get it to the cleaner. Now, don't give me a thought."

Finally, they left, with Penelope still protesting in one breath that too much was being made of a perfectly normal accident and bemoaning the ruin of her dress in another.

Susan dropped into a chair as the reaction to the events of the evening hit her. Penelope was a horror, but she was right about one thing and Susan had better face it. Eric would have to do a lot of entertaining, and she was blind. How could she reach for all the bright hopeful things Anne had held out to her if she couldn't even manage to eat properly? How could she help Eric get ahead? How could she possibly be his hostess? Feeling overwhelmed, she let the tears come, tears for all her dreams, tears of humiliation. How, oh how, could she go on with her life?

# Chapter Five

**S**usan had thought that she wouldn't be able to sleep when she finally went to bed, but she was so tired both physically and emotionally that she fell into a deep sleep almost at once.

When she opened her eyes the next morning, she thought that it was still the dark of night, and then she remembered that all her time was black. The building was quiet, and at first, she couldn't remember where she was; then it all came back, most especially the horror of dinner the night before.

How could she have let Eric down like that? How could she have been so clumsy? But then, in spite of her feelings of guilt, another thought came into her mind and wouldn't go away.

How could Eric have put her in such a position? At least he could have telephoned to ask if it would be all right for his mother to come. Had he known when he called that she was coming?

Then she remembered what Penelope had said. Eric had told her that morning that he was taking Susan out. How could he have been so sure of her?

"After all, we are engaged," she spoke aloud. "He'd have every right to expect me to go." But still, something inside her seemed to rebel at the thought of being taken so for granted. He could have asked what she wanted to do.

Well, it was done now, and she couldn't deny that she had been a complete flop at being a hostess. Hostess! Why she'd acted like the village idiot, and there was no getting around it.

A check of the clock told her that it was almost nine o'clock. She hadn't checked the time when she had gone to bed, but she knew she had slept a long time. Why not? She wasn't going anywhere, except maybe to the bathroom.

Feeling for her slippers and failing to find them, she padded across the carpeted floor to the bathroom. On the way, she realized that she was hungry. She would have to face the shambles that was her kitchen, whether she wanted to or not.

And it was a shambles. Dirty dishes, pots, and pans seemed to be everywhere.

Nothing was where she expected it to be. She reached for the kettle and found a pan still half full of barbecue sauce. Again, she tried for the kettle and almost knocked another pan off the stove.

In the first real fit of anger she had known since her blindness, she emptied the barbecue sauce into the garbage disposal, then threw the pan. It landed with a satisfying clang against the refrigerator, and she found that she felt better.

She had just washed the last of the pans when the doorbell rang.

Eric! Her heart sang, and she hurried to the door.

"Hi, it's Anne. I know I should have called, but--and this is the truth--I had an appointment in the next block, and he wasn't home; at least he didn't answer the door. I'm dying for a cup of coffee. Not very professional, but there it is."

"Come on in, and we'll have coffee as soon as I can find the kettle and the coffee too."

"No problem," Anne said as she entered. "The kettle's on the left-back burner and the coffees in the cabinet over the stove. I remember because that's where I keep mine."

"You mean they were there," Susan said, closing the front door.

"Were? Okay if I throw my coat on the couch?"

"Sure, go ahead. Yes, they were, but--Oh, Anne!" Suddenly, Susan was crying and trying to tell the whole awful thing, all at the same time.

"Hey, wait a minute until you get control of yourself," Anne said soothingly. "Sit down, and I'll take a look for the kettle. I have more practice than you do."

Susan could hear Anne moving around the kitchen, and then she heard a clang.

"Great, I found it. For some reason, it was on the shelf next to the sink."

"But that shelf's not wide enough for it," Susan said, drying her eyes.

"I know. What do you think the clang was? Hey, I didn't find the coffee, but I remembered where we put the jar with the tea bags and, bless our guardian angel, it's still there. Tea all right?"

"Sure."

"Now, for goodness sake, tell me what kind of army ran through this place. The water will boil in a few minutes."

The whistle had just sounded when Susan finished the whole story. Really, it wasn't quite so bad in the telling. Maybe because Anne was blind, she hadn't minded talking about it.

"I don't believe this!" Anne said when she had finished. "Do you mean she really talks like that? Oh, did she really put a bib on you? Susan, forgive me but--"

And she started to laugh, "And did you really tell her that she should have had a bib? Oh, I think that's fantastic! I wish I'd been here."

"I'm glad you think it was funny, and I wish you had been here. Maybe she'd have given you some of the attention." And to her amazement, she was laughing as hard as Anne.

"What did Eric do?" Anne's voice sounded more serious.

"What could he do?"

"Look, honey, I know I'm probably not being very professional, but I feel that you're my friend as well as my client, and I have to say this. There were a lot of things he could have done. For starters, he could have called you before they came prancing in here. I'm not criticizing him, but you have to put this thing into perspective. You weren't to blame. To this day, I avoid certain foods like the plague unless I'm in the privacy of my own home, and barbecued spareribs are one of them."

"But what could I do?" Susan asked. "I couldn't say, 'I don't want what you brought to eat.'"

"True. You were in a spot, but if you'll take my advice, and you don't have to, you'll have a talk with Eric. Tell him, for instance, how hard it is for you when someone takes over your kitchen. How well do you know his mother?"

"Not very well, really. She's usually in Florida all winter. Come to think of it, I don't know what she's doing home now."

"How did she treat you before you lost your sight?"

"I got the feeling that she was all for the marriage. Only, now--"

"Only, now she's not so sure?" Anne asked when Susan didn't finish the sentence.

"If you had a son who's a rising executive, would you want him to marry a blind woman?" Susan wanted to know.

"That's a question I can't answer objectively. Of course, I would, because I know that a blind woman can keep up her end of a marriage as well as anyone."

"Anne, I'm not sure that's true in this case. When I'm sitting here talking to you, I can laugh about what happened last night, but it wasn't funny."

"I know it wasn't. It must have been awful for you. But, really, she asked for it. I can't decide whether she's monumentally stupid or whether she really knew what she was doing."

"You can't mean you think she set me up. Oh, Anne, I can't believe it."

"I'll admit she doesn't sound quite that smart, but that devious, yes. I don't think in either case she knew just what would happen, and I guess that's why I think it's so funny that she got all that mess in her lap. Now, come on. We'll have our tea, and I'll call Judy. If she's free, she'll come over. It'll take eyes to get everything back where it belongs."

All day, Susan waited for Eric to call.

She didn't want to call him at the office, and she was even more reluctant to leave a message at home with Penelope. At six o'clock, the phone rang, and she was surprised to find that her hands were trembling as she reached for the receiver.

"Susan Perry."

"Hi, Susan Perry." Hearing Eric's voice, she was reminded of the night before. "Have you had a good day?"

"Not bad," she said. "Are you coming over?"

"Look, I'm sorry, but something's come up, and I just can't make it."

She never knew where she found the courage to say, "Can't or don't want to, Eric? I think we need to talk, and the longer we put it off, the harder it's going to be."

"I want to see you, Susan, but this is important. You know how it is."

"I'm sure you think it's important, but nothing is more important than our future."

"Aren't you being a bit dramatic? It is our future I'm thinking about. I may be on the spot for one of the biggest accounts I've ever landed. I know you don't want to stand in the way of that."

"I don't, of course, but can't it wait just a little while, just half an hour? Please, Eric."

"No, it can't wait. I'll be there tomorrow evening, and that's the best I can do. Now, gotta run."

And without giving her a chance to say a word, he hung up. She had been ready to replace the receiver when she heard a second click on the line. Someone had been listening, and it didn't take a lot of imagination to know who.

"Penelope!" she said and banged the receiver down.

The next day seemed endless. Susan tried to listen to the recorded book Anne had brought her the day before, but although she had found the book-jacket description interesting, she couldn't concentrate.

The volunteer who brought her midday dinner from Meals on Wheels told her it was a beautiful day:

"The kind of day that makes you want to drop everything and just go for a walk."

Susan could imagine the blue of the sky, probably broken here and there by small puffy clouds. She could imagine the oak tree beside her walkway as its new leaves began to grow tiny miracles of green--life and hope renewed. But where were life and hope for her?

Eric hadn't said anything about going out for dinner, so she made herself a chicken-salad sandwich from the carton Judy had brought when she had come to help restore the kitchen.

"We'll start on kitchen skills in a couple of days," Anne had promised when she left. "I'll get a volunteer to take you to the grocery store if you'd like to go."

At least the practical side of her new life was beginning to take shape, she thought as she washed her plate and cup. The rest of her, the part she thought of as her heart, for want of a better word, seemed to be permanently stuck in limbo.

The doorbell rang, and as soon as she opened the door, she knew it was Eric.

"Hi there," he greeted her and gave her a kiss on the cheek.

"My goodness, the wind is blowing. Give me your coat."

"That's okay. I don't have long. I have to get some paperwork done."

"Do you have time to sit down?" She knew it sounded petulant, but she didn't care.

He didn't seem to notice. "Sure, for just a few minutes. What have you been up to today? I like that dress. Is it new?"

"I bought it just before I went to the hospital, but you've said you like it before. Eric, what's wrong? I think I know, but I want to hear it from you."

"Give me a break, Susan. I'm working hard day and night. What's happened, anyhow? You didn't even ask how it's going. All this is for our future, you know."

"Is it?"

"Come on, you know it is. Stop feeling sorry for yourself. I know you've had a bad break, but it isn't my fault. Don't you ever think of anyone but yourself? Don't you ever stop to think what it means to me?"

"Of course I do. That's what I think we need to talk about." She was not going to cry, she wasn't!

"What's to talk about?" She could hear him putting his coat on. "I've told you, I'll stick by you, and I'm not the kind to go back on a bargain, no matter how inconvenient it may be to keep it. Now, come here and kiss me."

In spite of her determination to bring things out in the open, she found herself in his arms, being held safe and warm, at least for a while. He kissed her hard and released her.

"Now, let's not talk about this anymore."

"But, Eric, we need to talk about it, don't you see? It won't just go away because we don't talk about it. My blindness is a reality and more than an inconvenience."

"If you ask me, you're seeing too much of those people from that rehab place. Mother's right."

"What do you mean by that?"

"Just that she thinks they're giving you--well, false ideas. She thought you seemed a little hostile the night before last. You'll have to let us help you, darling."

"Help me! But, Eric, that's just it--"

"Listen, I've got to get going. Stop brooding about this. Mother and I are going to take care of you. In fact, she's going to call you with a proposition I hope you'll consider. Now, I'm off."

But Penelope didn't call. She presented herself at the door the next afternoon, just after Susan had finished her shower.

"I suppose I should have called," she told Susan, "but I thought it would be all right just to pop in on my way home from my bridge club."

"You almost found me in the shower," Susan said, holding out her hand for Penelope's coat.

"That's all right, honey, I'll just hang my coat in your little closet. You sit down."

Lord, give me the courage. Susan prayed as she moved in front of the coat closet and held out her hand again. "I'd rather do it myself. After all, you're my guest."

She took the coat--a fur that made her skin prickle--opened the closet, and placed it on a hanger.

"Well, aren't you a smart girl! Let's sit on the sofa. What a sweet little robe, but honestly, honey, it isn't your color."

Susan realized that she couldn't say a thing. She and Judy had gone shopping and bought the robe that day, so she didn't know whether that particular shade of blue was her color or not.

"I'll do some shopping for you. Maybe we can go through your things, and I can see what you need."

"That's nice of you, but please don't trouble."

"Listen to you! Trouble? It'll be no trouble at all. We want you pretty for our friends and Eric's business associates, now, don't we?"

"Yes, but I really won't be seeing any of them for a while."

"That's just what I want to talk to you about. I think, and Eric agrees, that you shouldn't be living here all by yourself. Honey, you're getting just the tiniest bit sulky, and I can't have that for my boy. So this is what we think would be best: You are coming to live with us."

"But I couldn't!"

"Now, you sweet little thing, of course, you can. We've got just oodles of room and think of the fun we'll have. Why I can give little dinners, and we'll show all our friends just how wonderful you are even though you're blind."

"I'll have to think about it," Susan finally managed to say in spite of the anger threatening to overflow. "I've hardly come home from the hospital, and I need time to put my life in order. I think it would be a mistake to do anything until I've adjusted a bit. It's awfully kind of you, but for now, no thank you."

"Of course, darling. You think about it for a couple of days, but don't take too long. I don't think you realize what an important man my son is."

"Your son and my fiancé. Yes, I do realize how important he is, and that's why I'll never stand in his way."

"Now, listen to me, Susan. We're not going to have it said that Eric ran out on you. You're going to stick to your bargain, just the same as he does. After all, the gain is all on your side.

I'd have thought you'd be grateful that he's still willing to marry you."

"I'm afraid you'll have to excuse me, Penelope." Susan knew she sounded like someone from an afternoon soap opera, but she didn't dare show any emotion; she just might explode. "I'm a bit tired," she added as she stood up.

"Of course you are, and I've just been going on and on. You think about things for a day or two, and you'll see it the way we do--I just know you will."

# Chapter Six

Susan sat listening to Penelope's quick steps click down the walk. The room was quiet, and when Penelope's car had purred away from the curb, Susan felt that she was the only person left alive in a dark landscape.

From a practical point of view, she was alone. If only she had someone to talk to! She needed to put her relationship with Eric and to herself into some kind of perspective.

Of course, there were Anne and Judy, but maybe Penelope and Eric were right. Maybe the people from the Department for the Visually Handicapped were giving her a false picture of what her life could be.

True, Anne was blind; but as Anne herself was always reminding her, they were different. Maybe she should move in with Eric and Penelope, but everything in her rebelled at the thought. Still, it was an answer and a comfortable one, she realized.

But do you really want a comfortable, easy answer? She asked herself. You know you'd never really know what you could do with your life.

But Eric is or will be my life, another part of her argued. His mother is a vital part of his life and should be a part of mine.

And this last was what she couldn't seem to reconcile. Penelope would always be there between them, and the thought surprised her with its simplicity and truth. Why hadn't she seen it before? Eric's life seemed to revolve around--no, to follow behind Penelope.

Do you want to fall in line? She asked herself.

What else can I do? The other part of her asked back. I'm blind. My work is gone.

My independence is gone.

And then the thought came: I might as well be dead.

Probably she had been pushing the thought away like an unwanted ugly dress for several days, and suddenly there it was. It would be easy for her, a doctor, to meet and give in to death.

She got up and went into the bathroom. Yes, there it was, the bottle of sleeping pills her doctor had prescribed for those nights when her headaches had kept her awake. It was easy to identify because it was the only prescription bottle in her medicine chest. Carefully, she took it from the shelf.

Most people made one of two mistakes: Either they didn't take enough of the drug, or they took too much and didn't keep it down. Well, she wouldn't fail. She knew her own tolerance and, therefore, just what the right dose would be.

She had always held a concealed contempt for those who chose suicide as the way out of problems they couldn't face, and now, she felt ashamed. How little she had known about the real sufferings of others. She had moved along through her existence without the slightest idea of what it was like to suffer, really suffer. Even when she had lost her parents, she had had her work to cushion her from the pain.

Now it seemed that all the pain, all the loneliness of those days, even the lonely days of her childhood in a home with middle-aged parents, hit her at once.

She couldn't go on. Her books had sustained her when she was a child, and later she had been able to hide inside her work. Now there was no hiding from the reality and the pain. Her books couldn't cushion the little girl who still cried for understanding, and her work was gone.

For a minute, she thought about calling Eric. No, she knew that Eric was as confused as she was. He couldn't help her. No one could help her. She started to count the pills. Suppose there weren't enough ... but there were, just.

Should she leave a note? No. She had always thought that such notes were melodramatic, to say the least. Everyone would know why. Surely they would understand that she couldn't go on.

She was startled by a voice coming from the bedroom. It was the clock announcing the hour.

Again, self-pity seemed to drown her. No one would really care. Of course, Eric and Penelope would pretend sorrow, but she knew that they would be relieved to get out of a situation they could not handle any more than she could.

The phone rang. She wouldn't answer ... but, no, that wasn't the thing to do. Whoever it was might get worried and come over. She would need several hours before she would be safe from efforts to revive her.

She cleared her throat--she'd have to sound normal--and went to answer the phone.

"Dr. Perry, this is Winifred Gordon.

Do you remember, from the clinic?"

Good. It was someone who didn't know her well enough to detect something wrong in her voice.

"Yes, Winifred. How are you?"

"I'm fine, doctor. I'm at the hospital, and--Oh, Dr. Perry, I have a baby girl! A beautiful little girl with Jim's eyes."

Oh, yes, now she really did remember Winifred--fair and fragile, with ankles horribly swollen from edema. Her husband had died in an accident of some sort at work just after the baby had been conceived. It had been touch and go, but Winifred had really wanted her baby.

"I don't care what I have to do, Dr. Perry--I have to have that baby," she had said then, and now it seemed that she had succeeded.

"I'm so glad, Winifred. Was it bad?"

"Not now it wasn't," the young woman replied, and Susan could imagine her smile. "I've almost forgotten what it was like."

Susan surprised herself by laughing; not, she realized, a stage laugh, but real joy.

"You know, it's usually like that," Susan said. "Most mothers, the ones who really want their babies, say it is."

Winifred laughed too.

"I guess it's like the psalm that says there'll be sorrow in the evening and joy in the morning. Well, it goes something like that. I never was very good at quoting the Bible, but I always liked that one."

Susan was remembering the birdlike woman who had taught her Sunday-school class, and she found herself smiling.

"Look, doctor, I didn't mean to keep you. I asked for you when I came in yesterday, and they said you'd been sick. I hope you're better now."

Of course, they wouldn't have told her anything more. "I'm going to be all right," Susan heard herself saying. "Is there anything I can do for you?"

What a stupid thing for her to say! She couldn't even help herself, and in a few hours, she would be beyond helping or help. It had been a reflexive question from doctor to patient.

"No, doctor, I just wanted to thank you. I honestly think I would have lost my baby if it hadn't been for you. You know that most of the other doctors at the clinic wanted me to have an abortion because of my health. You were just about the only one to agree that it was worth the chance. I'll never forget what you told me. I guess you don't remember since you see so many patients. But you told me that you had sworn to preserve life and that you weren't convinced it was necessary in my case to take it. The others didn't seem to think of my baby as life. Oh, I know that's not true, but you seemed to understand that my baby was a person, a part of Jim. You even gave me your number so I could call you at home if the going got rough."

"Yes, I remember." And now, there were tears in Susan's eyes.

"Are you okay, Dr. Perry?"

"Sure, but I think someone's at my door. Take good care of that little girl, and call me again."

Susan knew that if she said another word, she would start to cry, and she had offered the classic excuse to get away from a caller.

"Sure will," Winifred said. "Take care, and thank you."

Susan dropped her head on the table beside the telephone and gave way to the tears. She had sworn to preserve life and had fought against death. Was it different now? Did she have the right to take a life even if it was her own? Would joy follow the sorrow of her lonely night?

She knew she was getting fanciful. It wasn't really unusual for one of her clinic patients to call to tell her that she had delivered; it happened fairly often. Still, this call had been timed just right.

The conversation, too, hadn't been awfully different from many others. She had marveled at the faith that had sustained many of her patients. Well, it had certainly been the right call at the right time--or maybe the wrong time, depending on how she looked at it.

Slowly she went back to the bathroom. She picked up the bottle of sleeping pills, emptied the capsules into the toilet, and flushed.

Back in the living room, she stood thinking and then punched a button on the phone. Her hands were trembling, but her voice was almost normal when she said, "Anne, I need you."

Anne had made the coffee. By the time she had rang the doorbell, Susan had found that she was shaking so much that she could hardly make it to the door.

"No," Anne said, "we're not going to talk. Sit down here on the couch. I'll get us some coffee, and then we'll talk."

"And that's it," Susan said a few minutes later, as she set her mug on the coffee table. "I know it sounds like something from a revival meeting, but that's what happened."

"No, it doesn't. Personally, I believe in a higher power that moves in our lives, but whether I do or not, this makes sense. You would have found something to stop you if that phone call hadn't come."

"No, Anne, I meant to do it. I'm not proud of my weakness, but I really did mean to kill myself."

"Oh, sure, part of you couldn't see any other way out, but I still say you didn't mean to do it. You seized too quickly on what that girl said. If you had really meant to end your life, you would have thanked her for calling and heard someone at the door as soon as she started to talk. Something would have stopped you if she hadn't called. Of course, she did put her finger on the reason you wouldn't ever kill yourself. You're a fighter, and that part of you is strong."

"Oh, Anne, I wish I were a fighter, but I'm not. I'm a professional woman, and I'm acting like a kid not out of high school. I know I should take charge of my life, but I just can't."

"But don't you see you are taking charge? You knew that what you were going to do wasn't the answer, and you latched on to the logic of not doing it. You knew, too, that I was probably the right person to help you, and you called me."

"But why can't I help myself?"

"None of us could in the circumstances you're facing. Your whole life, or way of life, has crumbled. I don't have to tell you how hard it is to cope with that. You're a doctor. How many times have you helped someone, not through just the same thing, but through something similar?"

"Well, obviously a lot of times, but that's just my point. Why can't I help myself?"

"Why couldn't those people you helped do it? Do you think you're smarter than they were?"

"Certainly, I'm better equipped to do it," Susan said.

"Sure, I'll give you that. But, honey, the truth is--and you know this--we just can't always see our way around our own problems. Let's leave that part of it for now. Just take my word that you're not to blame because you can't stand all by yourself right now. Okay?"

"Okay. At least I see what you're getting at. Maybe you're right, too, when you say I would have come up with the reason to stop myself if Winifred hadn't called. But, Anne, what am I going to do, about Eric, I mean?"

"What do you want to do?" Anne asked, taking Susan's cup along with her own to the kitchen for more coffee.

"I don't know," Susan said, taking the cup. "I know I can't do what he and his mother want me to do, but I'm not sure that I should just give up and tell him to get lost."

"No, I think that wouldn't be the thing. You'd never know whether something could have been salvaged. It comes down to the classic situation of a strong mother figure, and--forgive me, Susan--a weak personality. He may love you very much, but the habit of following after his mother is just too strong. He may simply not know how to break away."

"And," Susan said, "He may actually believe that it would be the best thing for me to let her take care of me."

"I was going to point that out. Do you think it would be a good idea for someone from our department to have a talk with him? One of the guys, I think. He has to resent Penelope on some level, and that resentment can include all women. I'd just put him off."

"I honestly don't know. He doesn't seem to have accepted my blindness as a reality. When I try to talk to him about it, he always turns away in one way or another."

"Do you think he would resent someone having a talk with him? We often talk to those who are close to the client. It wouldn't be anything special in your case."

"I'm confused," Susan said. "I don't know what to think about anything."

"You're tired. You've had a dickens of a time for the last few days. You're the doctor. You could tell me all kinds of symptoms such an experience could cause. Just try to relax."

They sat in silence. Outside, the wind had risen, and frozen rain clicked at the window. On the street, cars swished their way along in the night. Susan could imagine their lights appearing and disappearing, only to be replaced with others, and still others.

Finally, Anne spoke.

"I'm going to make a suggestion. I haven't really thought it out, but let's at least look at it."

"Sure," Susan said. "I think I'm open to almost anything at this point."

"I would have talked to you about this eventually, but normally I would have waited until you were stronger-- physically,

I mean. After tonight, though, I feel that you need a little extra support right now.

"We have a rehab center. You would learn all kinds of personal skills--cooking, housekeeping, communication skills, and the works. Some folks take job training there, but we're not thinking about that just now."

"I know I need all those things, but I'll have to tell you the truth--it scares me to think about it. Are you sure it isn't too soon?"

"No, I'm not sure," Anne admitted, "but if the counselors there find that it is, you can always come home and go again later. I don't think it is too soon, though. As we've already said, you're a fighter, and it might be that you're getting bored with nothing to fight but yourself."

"You said, "Come home." I'd stay there, then?"

"Yes. The time would vary according to what you were doing, but we could count on at least a month, and probably longer. We wouldn't want to push you physically. Of course, your doctor would have to give his okay before we could do anything."

"Could I think about it?" And Susan was reminded of her earlier conversation with Penelope.

"I want you to think about it. If you said you wanted to go, I'd still tell you to think about it. You shouldn't go just to get away from this spot Penelope has put you in, but it will get you off the hook until you can get a handle on your life. Take as much time as you need. Just promise you'll call me if you really get bogged down with the thinking. I don't want this to make you feel trapped. Remember, it's your life, and you're in charge of it."

"I'd like to ask you something, Anne." Susan's mouth felt dry. "Do you think I'm the wrong woman for Eric?"

Anne was silent for a long moment. Then she said, "If you mean do I think you're the wrong woman because you're blind--no, I don't. You've already started making a great adjustment, and I'll admit I can hardly wait to get you to the rehab center. I'm dying for you to see what you can do."

"But what else could there be? I mean, what other consideration could there be except my blindness? Of course, I'm the right woman, if I could only see."

Then Anne said the words Susan was to hear over and over: "But you can't see. And forgive me, Susan, you have to accept it--accept it, and go on up from there. Now, if you think I'm going out in that weather, you're dead wrong. Where's your linen closet? It's your couch for me tonight."

# Chapter Seven

Susan lay listening to the icy rain blowing against the windows. Few cars moved now, and except for a dripping faucet in the bathroom, the apartment, too, was quiet.

She wondered what time it was, but hesitated to check her talking clock for fear of waking Anne. She would be glad when her Braille watch came. Anne had ordered it the day she came home from the hospital.

"Your clock is fine when you're at home, but a watch can go anywhere," Anne had explained to her.

How many things she had always taken for granted, she thought as she lay listening to the rain. She had, for instance, never given the means of telling time a thought before she lost her sight. What a help Anne was in so many ways!

"Won't your family need you?" she had asked when Anne had announced that she was going to spend the night. Susan hadn't been fooled for a minute by her protest about going out in the rain. It wasn't that Anne didn't trust her, she was sure of that. No, she had thought that Susan might need further support before morning.

"My family?" Anne had said in answer to her question. "You gotta be kidding! The kids will be thrilled. Chet always reads more to them than I do, and they love anything to put off going to sleep."

"Then, won't your husband miss you?"

"Miss, yes, but if you mean can he manage with the kids--he likes spoiling them as much as they liked being spoiled. Now quit fussing, and let's get this bed made."

Susan found herself wondering what it would be like to have a home and children. She realized with surprise that that had been something she and Eric had never talked about. Somehow, she had always taken children for granted as a natural part of marriage, but did Eric?

Then she realized they had never talked much about the future except how their careers would relate to it. They had never talked about where they would live, and now she wondered if all along, Penelope and Eric had planned on their living with her.

She thought about her own mother: plump, middle-aged, and obviously--even to the young Susan--madly in love with Susan's father. Would she and Eric be like that in, say, twenty years?

Twenty years. She and Eric would be well into their forties. How old her parents had seemed, and how really short a time twenty years would be! No matter how hard she tried, though, she couldn't imagine sitting quietly by the fire with Eric, seeing who-knew-what visions in the flames.

Their time together had been filled with restaurants, dancing, and all Eric's plans for the future. Strange that now she couldn't imagine what that future would be like, and not for the first time she wondered if they had a future together.

She would have to get to sleep. She was almost exhausted physically, but she couldn't seem to turn off her thoughts. No matter how she tried, they kept on running around and around, like a kitten busy chasing its own tail.

What should she do about going to the rehab center? She knew that it would mean a lot to her, but would she be just using it as an excuse to get out of the situation she found herself in with Eric and Penelope?

Did Eric really think that it would be better for her to move in with Penelope, or was he just giving in, as always? She suddenly knew that whether she went to the center or not, she would not, could not move in with them. It would be a big mistake for both her and Eric. Of course, she knew, Penelope would love having them live with her. Apparently, she had been "head of the family" for years. What an old-fashioned term! Susan almost laughed to think what Penelope would say if she were called that, but it was a good description. Eric's father had died when Eric was five, and apparently, Penelope had never even thought about marrying again.

"Well, my dear, you know I had my little man," she had told Susan one evening during dinner at the big old brick house where Penelope and Eric lived.

Now Susan wondered how she could have been so stupid as not to have seen how possessive the woman was. No, there was no way she could live in the same house with Penelope, and Eric would have to accept it.

And she fell asleep wondering what life at the rehab center would be like.

"Wake up, the sun is shining!" Anne almost sang the words.

"Is it morning?" Susan asked. She had been sure that she would lie awake all night.

"Hungry?" Anne asked. Susan was aware of the smell of freshly perked coffee and something else. ...

"Bacon!" she said and threw back the covers.

"Hope you don't mind," Anne said. "I looked around in your freezer unit and found it. You know, Penelope's right."

"She is?" Susan stopped dead on her way to the bathroom.

"You do need a microwave, Susan, my dear." Both women laughed. "Honestly, you do," Anne said. "It's the easiest way I've found to fix bacon. I'll check, and if we have one in our supplies for clients, I'll bring it over."

"I don't think it'll be necessary, not right now at least. Anne, I want to go to the rehab center."

"All right, but are you sure?"

"Is anyone ever absolutely sure?" Susan asked.

"Not really. I wanted to go one minute, and the next, I couldn't stand the thought. It was sort of like when I was getting ready to go off to college my freshman year. I wanted to go, knew I had to go, and at the same time, I was afraid to break that final link with childhood. You'll get over all that as soon as you get there. You'll be too busy wondering what you're going to learn next, and if you do think about it, you'll wonder why you ever had doubts."

"It's funny," Susan said, drying her hands, "but somehow, I feel more in control of things this morning. Is that a passing thing too? I mean, will I find myself teetering between being in control and giving in to dear Penelope?"

"I doubt it," Anne replied. And Susan could hear her setting plates on the table. "It's funny, but it seems that once you've made a definite decision or taken a definite stand, you do feel more in control. Oh, I'm not saying that you won't doubt your judgment and ability, but that's human. We all do whether we're blind or not. Didn't you have doubts when you could see?"

"Well, yes, but--"

"It's the same thing, only now you have the added pressure of knowing that you're blind. One of the worst things about being blind is that people have a way of reducing us to children. If we go along with it, we're like children in our own sight, if you'll pardon the pun. Come and have breakfast."

"You know, you're right," Susan said after they were seated at the counter. "About us feeling like children, I mean. I hadn't thought about it, but that's just the way I've felt. I can't really explain it, but that's what it's been like. I've actually been afraid to make decisions."

"Yes, and I'll expect that you were afraid, at least subconsciously, to voice any real opinion. How Penelope must have loved that! Well, the old girl had better be warned that the fun's over. You're on your way."

Susan sat finishing her coffee after Anne had gone. She knew she would have to tell Eric what she had decided, and everything in her cringed at the thought.

Could Eric have started thinking of her as a child? Anne had told her that people often did that even though they weren't aware of it. Well, it was up to her to change his mind.

Then she had an idea. At first, she rejected it. She couldn't do it--she knew she couldn't--but the thought wouldn't go away.

Suppose she tried and failed. Well, what if she did? She wouldn't lose anything except her dignity, and she had already lost that the other night.

She went to the telephone and pushed a button before she lost her nerve.

"This is Dr. Perry," she said. "I'd like to speak to Mr. Graham if he's free."

"Dr. Perry, how nice it is to hear your voice. I'll see if he's free; hold, please."

Part of her hoped he would be with a client, while the other part of her almost prayed that he would be free.

There was a click, and Eric said, "Susan?"

"Good morning. Are you free for lunch? If you are, I thought I could meet you at Selbys."

"As a matter of fact, I am free. But really, Susan, do you think you're up to it?"

"I'm absolutely sure. I have something to tell you, and I've been shut up here too long. I need to get out."

"Why don't I pick up something, and--"

"No, Eric," she said, fighting against the need to agree. "I'm perfectly able to come out. Is twelve-fifteen all right?"

"I'm not sure--I suppose so." "Good. And, Eric, please don't be angry, but I want this to be just us. Don't feel that I need your mother there."

"I'm sure she'd be glad. ..." He didn't seem to know how to finish the sentence.

Then she surprised even herself. "I'm sure she would be glad, but as I told you, I don't need her. And, darling, neither do you. See you."

As she stood waiting for her taxi an hour later, she wondered if she was slightly out of her mind. Going out alone was such a big thing. Of course, if everything went well, she would have scored a big point, but suppose. ... She wouldn't let herself think about that.

She had told the dispatcher at the taxi company to tell the driver that his passenger was blind, and to her surprise, he seemed glad to pass the word on. Apparently, he had such requests often. That was another thing she had never even thought about before her blindness.

She knew it was her taxi by the sound of the two-way radio.

"Good morning," a friendly middle-aged-sounding voice said, and an elbow was thrust against her arm. "Take my arm?"

"Yes, thank you." And thank you too, God, she said silently as the driver guided her down her walk.

"The door's open--just you slide right in. Where are we going?"

"To Selbys on Main Street." She settled back. If only her heart wasn't beating so fast.

When they reached Selbys, the clock at the Presbyterian Church was striking the quarter-hour.

"Here comes a nice-looking boy, and I bet he's coming to meet you."

"How much?" she asked, opening her purse. She was grateful to Judy for helping her fold her bills so she could identify the different denominations. She added a dollar tip to the amount the driver named and then stepped forward to where the smell of after-shave told her Eric was waiting.

"Hi," she said, holding out her hand.

"Hi, yourself." He took her hand, then just stood there.

"Give me your arm, and just walk along the way you usually do. I promise I won't break."

All the way over in the taxi she had been thinking about what to order, finally deciding on the chef's salad. She knew from experience that it was good, and best of all, it would be easy to manage.

"This is quite a surprise," Eric said when they had been served.

"I hope a pleasant surprise." Oh, she sounded stilted and formal, but he didn't seem to notice.

"Of course. But really, Susan, should you be out by yourself?"

"Darling, I'm not by myself, you're here." How dumb that sounded!

"You know what I mean, traveling alone. ..." He let the sentence drop.

Probably he didn't know what else to say, she thought and hated herself for thinking that.

"I'm perfectly safe. Isn't the coffee good today? Eric, I have something I want to talk to you about, and I know you don't have a lot of time, so I think I'd better get right to it."

"Well, sure, but--"

He was having trouble knowing what to say. She wondered if he'd always been that way, and she hadn't really noticed.

"I'm going to be gone for a while. I'm going to the Rehab Center for the Visually Handicapped in Richmond."

He didn't say anything, but she knew he'd stopped eating. She'd heard him put his fork down.

"I really think it's the best thing for me to do. There are so many things I need to learn. And, to tell the truth, I think we both need time to do some thinking."

"Thinking about what?"

"I don't mean to hurt you, but, Eric, are you sure you want to spend the rest of your life with a woman who can't see?"

"I've already told you, Susan. I stand by my bargains."

"That's not what I asked you, Eric. I know you won't walk out on me; both you and your mother have told me so several times. No, the question is: Do you want me? I feel that I owe it to you, and for that matter, to myself, to give you a chance to make an honest decision, one based not on what you think is the right thing, but on what you, and only you, really want."

There was a large lump in her throat, making it hard to speak, but she had managed to say what she had to say. She prayed she wouldn't cry.

"Susan, what's the matter? I've told you, we're going on with our plans for our wedding in December. If you insist, then go to this place, but I think it's foolish. As Mother said last night, she's perfectly able to advise and help you. Susan, you have to believe that; she really wants to help you."

"Yes, Eric, I do believe that she wants to help, but what neither of you seem to understand is that the kind of help I need is to be allowed to learn to start living my life again. No matter how much she wants me there, your mother's home isn't, and never can be, my home."

"I'm trying to understand, but you're not making it easy," he said. "You've had a bad break, but you're lucky to have Mother, willing to give up her life to help us with ours. We'll have to do a lot of entertaining if I'm going to get ahead. Darling, no matter how much you want to, you can't do it."

Her new-found courage almost deserted her at that point, but she knew she'd have to go on.

"You may be right, Eric, but that's something that neither of us knows for sure. Give me a chance to put things in order. Give me a chance to see just what I can do; then we'll decide."

She held out her hand, and he took it. "Oh, Susan! If you could only be right ... but darling, you'll have to accept the fact that nothing is the same. I know they've told you about all the things you'll be able to do, and I'm sure that they're right to a point. Still--Oh, well, we'll wait and see. Go take your training or whatever it is. Just remember that Mother and I will be waiting when you come back."

She didn't let go until she reached home. Then she cried for about ten minutes and was surprised to find that when she'd washed her face, she felt better.

As she poured boiling water over a teabag, she knew that Eric was right about at least one thing. They would have to wait until she was finished at the center and then decide.

She put a tape on the stereo. She couldn't think about what that decision might mean, but she knew that at least she would be able to make it when the time came.

She had been so afraid to leave the safety of her apartment for the trip to the restaurant, a thing most people did every day without giving it a thought. Yes, her life had certainly changed. But for the first time, she felt that she could accept that change.

# Chapter Eight

There was no spring that year. March had promised warm sun and soft rain, only to go back on its word by dumping six inches of snow on the trusting young green things. April and May were a little better, with cold rain driven by a wind that seemed more typical of November. Then it was summer, with no rain and a sun that parched the land and refused to let the plants grow.

Susan paid little attention to this betrayal of nature. Every day for her seemed filled with magic, as her new world opened before her. Of course, it was actually the old world, but a world she had thought she would never have again. Because she had to think about every action, things seemed bigger, and when the victory came, it meant so much. She never stopped marveling at how she had taken her world so much for granted.

At the end of the first month, there was no chance that she would go back home. She had barely scratched the surface of that big new world of darkness turned to light. They couldn't have forced her to leave.

As the summer moved through July and August and September began, she found that she thought less and less about Eric. The days were so full, and the nights were filled with sound sleep that there was no room left--or so it seemed to her.

They corresponded at first, but although she could write letters to him by using the typewriter, his letters sounded— forced, probably because he knew that they would have to be read aloud to her. She had suggested that they use tape recorders for correspondence, but somehow he never seemed to get around to it.

Once, he and Penelope came to see her, but Susan felt like a little girl whose parents have come to visit at summer camp, and she was really glad when they left. They didn't belong there in that world of struggle, victory, and sometimes failure. She knew, of course, that one day soon, she would have to put those two worlds together to make the whole of her life, but she found that she didn't want to think about that day.

It was the second week in September when Ted, the director, called her to his office, and to her surprise, she found Anne there too.

"Hey," Susan said, giving her a hug, "I've missed you."

"Me too," Anne said. "I haven't got a single place to get a cup of coffee when Mr. Smith runs out on his appointment. How are things going?"

"Great. I went shopping all by my lonesome yesterday. The only thing I collided with was a horse."

"You know, I think Richmond keeps its mounted police just to give the clients at the rehab center a chance to tell everybody they bumped into a horse."

Susan laughed. "I bet the horses would miss us."

"I asked Anne to join us today," Ted said, "because she found the proposition we're going to make you. Well, that sentence sounds mixed."

"What he means," Anne said, "is that we have a job that we think might interest you, and I'm the one who ran across it while I was visiting a client."

"I really hadn't thought much about a job," Susan confessed. "I guess medicine was such a big thing in my life for so long that I'm resisting the thought that my professional life will have to go on without it."

"But that's the beauty of this job." Susan could tell by the enthusiasm in her voice that Anne was off and running.

"Anne, I don't know. You know I'm planning to be married in December."

"Yes, and for that reason, I almost didn't tell you about this. I held off, as a matter of fact, until I came down here for a staff meeting. I just couldn't make up my mind whether we should say anything, but it's perfect for you."

"She didn't mention your name to me," Ted said. "She just described the situation to me, and my first words were, 'Let's talk to Susan.'"

"Let me tell you about it," Anne said. "You don't have to decide here on the spot. Muddle it around for a while; talk to Eric. You know we're not trying to pressure you."

"I might," Ted said, lighting his pipe. "Pressure you, I mean. I'll be honest with you, Susan. You've done so well here that I'd like to see you have the independence of a job for a while before you're married."

Susan had to admit to herself that lately, she'd been thinking about those days with nothing to do except wait for Eric to come home at night, but she wasn't going to reveal her fears to anyone, not even Anne.

"All right," she said. "I'll listen, but I won't make any decision now."

"Fair enough," Anne said. "Well, as I told you, I was visiting a client way out in the middle of nowhere, and I mean nowhere. I had to get a driver with a four-wheel drive. You wouldn't believe the roads. Anyway, my client told me that the area is getting a clinic. The nearest hospital is thirty-five miles away, and last year the doctor who had taken care of people in her area died. Well, it seems that the local boy who made well--in oil, I think--gave the land and a substantial amount of money for a clinic."

"Now wait, Anne--"

"You promised to listen, and already you're jumping to conclusions. To get back to my tale--the good old boy then donated enough money to pay the salaries of staff until the thing can fly on its own. They're looking for a social worker--nothing grand--and before you start objecting, you qualify. I've already looked into that. In fact, I'll have to confess, I've given your credentials to the doctor in charge, and he's dying to get you if you're as good as I say."

"Susan"--Ted's voice sounded serious-- "this wouldn't ask for anything that you're not more than capable of delivering. Your work would consist mainly of interviewing patients and helping them with any problems, financial mostly, that they might have.

You'd determine eligibility for Medicaid, and make the referral to the proper agency--things like that. We're not suggesting that you practice medicine."

"I'm not a social worker," Susan protested. "Of course, I took courses in psychology. But I don't know whether I could do the job, even if I decide I'd like to try."

"Neither do we, really." Anne was serious now as she added, "But Dr. Monroe feels that you can. The way I understand it, an ability to get along with people is more important to him than how many courses you've had."

"Of course, I've had clinic experience, and I'll have to admit that I enjoyed that part of my residency. I always felt that I needed to understand the whole patient, not just her medical problems. Oh, I don't know. It sounds like a bad area for a blind person to live."

"I'll admit that," Anne said. "That was one of the things I brought up when I talked to Dr. Monroe. I was concerned about living arrangements. After all, the subway doesn't exactly rumble along under the next street over. The clinic is in an old converted mansion, of all things, and there is an apartment upstairs."

"No doubt the housekeeper's rooms,"

Susan said, laughing.

"You know, I honestly think it was. You might get lonely, though, Sue, and that is something that you will have to think about. The other folks on the staff seem like nice young people, but you would be pretty much on your own in the evenings."

"I really don't think that would bother me. I finally have the time to read, and it's a joy. I could take my stereo. No, I don't think I'd mind that part of it. I like my own company."

"All right," Anne said, "think about it. Dr. Monroe says that finding the right person is more important to him than getting one right away."

"If you're at all interested," Ted said, "I'll drive you over for an interview. After all, you may find that you and Monroe can't stand each other, and that would finish the thing there."

But that hadn't been the case.

A week later, Susan and Ted had made the trip through the autumn-filled landscape. They drove with the windows open, and Susan caught the smells of burning leaves and ripening apples.

Dr. Monroe could almost be called old, but he was full of enthusiasm. Susan found herself falling under the spell of both the man and the clinic.

"You have no idea what this place means to the people of the area," he told her. "When Dr. Wilson died last year, there was absolutely no medical help closer than Windburg, thirty-five miles over the mountain."

"Are you an inpatient facility?" She was becoming interested in spite of herself and found that she was falling into old habits of speaking and thinking.

"No, and we probably won't be, at least not for years. No, our aim is to provide everyday and emergency care. If we're faced with a really big emergency, we can call on the helicopter. So far, thank the Lord, we haven't had to, but it's good to know it's there."

"What's the economic status of most of your patients?" Susan asked.

"Most falls below the poverty level, I'm afraid. That's why we need someone who has a real way with people to fill this post. You can live in this place for fifty years, and some of the old-timers still think of you as an outsider."

"I'm going to be honest with you, Dr. Monroe. I'm not sure that I'm the person you want."

"And I'll be honest with you, Dr. Perry. I'm not sure I know just what the right person is like. My last practice was in an area very much like this one, so I'm fairly familiar with the problem, but I don't pretend to understand what makes our patients tick. In the end, though, they're like people everywhere, good and bad; only, here there are no really rich ones."

"How do you think they would feel about me? A blind woman, I mean."

"You won't be offended?"

Susan shook her head.

"All right, here goes. I think it would be an asset. Many of them are proud. I mean really proud--the kind of proud that would almost rather starve or die for lack of medical attention than say they can't afford it. Somehow I have the feeling they'll find it easier to come to you with their needs."

"Why?"

"You tell me. Think for a minute."

"You mean," she said slowly, "they won't mind quite so much exposing their weakness to someone they feel has a greater weakness?"

"Exactly. They won't feel sorry for you; at least most of them won't. They'll admire you, and something may say to them that if you've overcome your trouble, well, maybe they can too."

"Yes, I can see that. In a way, it's the same thing that often makes a woman obstetrician more effective, or a blind rehab worker, come to think of it. It's--oh, I don't know--a feeling that this person has been there."

"You've got it. Of course, I could be wrong, but leaving all that out of it, I think you would be a great addition to our staff. There is one other thing before we get down to discussing salary."

There was always one other thing, and she sighed inwardly.

"There will be some traveling--to homes, I mean. Would that bother you?"

She was surprised at how disappointed she felt. She hadn't known how much she had wanted at least to give the job a try until he mentioned something that would be an impossibility. There was no way she could travel in a rural area with no public transportation.

"I've learned to travel independently, but that's in an area where one can get public transportation if it's too far to walk. I wouldn't mind, but rural traveling would be impossible."

"Oh, I know that. We would help you find drivers, of course."

She felt her heart give a little lurch of what she could only call joy. "In that case, of course, traveling would be no problem at all."

She hardly listened as he explained about the salary.

Outside, the September wind rustled leaves, and far off a dog barked and howled. A car door closed in the parking lot, and she heard a baby cry. And for the first time since she had known that she would never see again, her heart felt at peace.

"I'll think about it," she told Dr. Monroe as he took her hand across his desk.

"I'll pray you think yes," he said. "I can honestly say that you seem perfect for the job. We'll be more than lucky if you'll come."

"I'll think about it," she said again, but deep inside she knew that in spite of her fears of a job, in spite of the isolation of the place and the possible strangeness of the people, in spite of her commitment to Eric--in spite of all these things and more, she would say yes.

"Well?" Ted said, helping her into the car. "I said I'd think about it, but I think I'd like to try."

"I thought you might. They really do need you, Susan. Remember, they'd be indebted to you--not the other way around."

"I hope so," she said.

As they turned onto the main road, she fastened her seat belt and was soon fast asleep.

# Chapter Nine

Eric met her at the airport the next afternoon. "You look happy," he said as he took her flight bag. "You've changed your hairstyle. I like it."

"So do I." She took his arm.

"Give me your claim checks, and I'll get the rest of your things."

"This is all," she said.

"I thought you were coming home to stay."

"No. To tell the truth, Eric, I came to talk to you and to do a few things at the apartment."

"Susan, at first you said you'd be gone a month. That was the first of April, and this is September. What's with you?"

She could hear the amusement in his voice and imagined his smile, that smile that had been able to make the day smile for her.

"Let's get to the car first, and I'll tell you."

"You are going to go where, and do what?" he exclaimed when she had told him.

"You heard me. Oh, Eric, please try to understand. I'm not telling you that we're not going to be married; I'm just asking you to give me a year. After all, you had reservations about December in the first place. Remember?"

"Well, yes, but that was because I thought it might be better for us to get ahead a bit more. Now all that's changed."

"I don't see what the difference is. I won't be making a fabulous salary, but since they're furnishing my apartment, I'll be able to save more than I would have just started out in practice."

"My wife doesn't have to work."

"Eric, we agreed that it was the thing to do. Look, if I get experience in this place, I'll probably be able to find a job next year in the D.C. area. I'll admit that I was wrong to make up my mind without talking to you first, but I have to do it, and I guess I thought you'd understand."

"It isn't that I don't understand, and you know I don't think that you shouldn't make your own decisions. It's just that I don't think this is the kind of thing you should be doing. You say this place is somewhere near Windburg?"

"About thirty-five miles from there," she said. "I know that area. We did an ad campaign for a firm that was thinking about opening a plant there. It's a backwoods place if I ever saw one. You can't seriously be thinking about working and living there."

"Yes, I can. I have to start someplace, and I think the work will be interesting. Eric, I'm sorry about the way I've handled this. We should have talked it over. Forgive me?"

"That has nothing to do with it, Susan. How can I tell people that I've let you go way out to the back of beyond to work with a lot of dirty hillbillies?"

"Eric, that's unfair! You have no more idea of what those people are like than I have. Dr. Monroe did tell me that most of their patients are below the poverty level, but I don't know anything else."

"Isn't that enough to make my point? I suppose I can't talk you out of this?"

"That depends. I don't think your reasons for not wanting me to take the job are very good ones. I've already said I was sorry for not talking to you before I made up my mind, but I thought I knew what your attitude would be."

"What other reasons could I have for not wanting you to take the job? Look, if you have to work, Mother does a lot of volunteer work. The offer to move in with us is still good. Why not let me take you back to Richmond tomorrow to get the rest of your things? We can store your furniture and things you won't need until you decide what you want to do with them. You could be in that nice big corner room at the house by tomorrow night. You and Mother could do work together."

She shook her head. "I'm sorry. I have to do this. I have to prove to myself that I can."

If he'd only told me that he'd miss me, that he was disappointed because I wanted to postpone our marriage, she thought, I'd have ditched the job in a minute.

They hardly talked for the rest of the drive to her apartment.

"I'm sorry I can't come in," he said, putting her bag on the floor inside the front door. "I have a meeting in an hour."

"All right," she said, and they just stood there. She wanted him to take her in his arms. She wanted and needed the comfort of his lips on hers.

"When will you be going back?" he asked.

"Probably late tomorrow. I'll leave for the job from there. I'll try to get back in a month or so. By then I'll know where I stand--with the job, I mean. I suppose I should try to find someone to finish out my lease here."

"I'll see you when you get back, then. I have appointments through dinner tomorrow. Take care, Susan, and don't worry--everything's all right."

He had said the words she had been wanting to hear ever since she had told him about the job. He did understand. He did know how much she needed reassurance in spite of her outward confidence.

"Thank you, darling," she said, holding up her face for the kiss she so wanted and needed.

"Mother and I will think of something to tell our friends. Don't worry. No one will know what you're really doing."

She let her arms drop to her side, and tried to control the anger and tears that were threatening to control her.

"All right, Eric," she said tensely, and she closed the door before she threw her purse across the room. Anger had won over tears.

When the telephone rang early the next morning, she was sure it must be Eric. She was wrong.

"Susan, my dear, this is Mother Graham." She's rushing things a bit, Susan thought as she said, "Penelope, what a surprise!"

Well, that wasn't a lie. She just didn't say what kind of surprise.

"Did I wake you up, darling?"

"No, I've been up for an hour or so. I have a lot of things to get done today."

"I know you must be busy. Eric's told me about your little plan."

Here we go, Susan thought, putting her cup of coffee on the floor beside her chair. It wouldn't do to throw that across the room. "Yes?" she said into the receiver.

"I think it's just marvelous," Penelope trilled. "I mean, as I told Eric, you have to do something. And really, Susan honey, I think you're smart to make my good, kind boy give himself

71

some extra time before you're married. You're a thoughtful, dear girl, really you are."

"Yes, I know."

Had she really said that?

"What did you say, darling?"

Yes, she had.

"I said yes--yes, we, he needed more time."

"Now, what I wanted to tell you, Susan is not to worry about a thing. I'll take good care of Eric. You just go and have a good time."

"That's hardly the reason I'm going, Penelope--to have a good time, I mean. I am going to work, remember?"

"I know, darling, and, honestly, I think they're so good at that place to give you a little something to do. We all need that. I told Eric last night, 'Now, you just leave little Susan alone about getting married right away, and don't try to make her give up this idea. She needs to feel important.'"

"Yes, well, thank you for calling, Penelope. I hear someone at the door. I have to go."

"All right, darling. Now, don't worry, and maybe we'll just surprise you and come up there someday to see you."

"Yes, well, good-bye."

"Bye, now," she chirped as Susan replaced the receiver and kicked something.

"Oh, blast!" She had kicked her cup of coffee.

Susan arrived at the clinic on a day of flying leaves and warm sun. She had flown in the medical helicopter from Byrde Field to the little airstrip at Windburg.

"No problem," the pilot said in response to her thanks. "We took a patient to the medical college last night. Doc Monroe knew we were going and told us to see if you needed a lift."

"It sure beats the bus and the drive from the terminal," she said.

"Doc said he was planning to meet you at the bus, but you got here in style. Here's Doc now. Got her here," he shouted, although Susan could tell by the approaching footsteps that the shout wasn't necessary.

"Thanks, Harry. Did you get word of Simons before you left?"

"Doing fine, the nurse in the burn unit said. They're pretty sure he'll make it, the fool. Imagine cleaning the shop floor with gasoline."

"Our first removal by the bird," Dr. Monroe told her as she settled in the front seat of his car.

"Burns are nasty things," she said. "What's headquarters for the copter?"

"Charlottesville. They don't carry passengers, of course, but the rest of the staff went back to Charlottesville last night. There was some minor problem with the copter, and Harry had to stay over. We all help each other around here."

It was Saturday afternoon, and although the clinic was closed, the staff was waiting to meet her.

As she went through the heavy front door, Susan could smell coffee and the faint scent of disinfectant. It smelled good; it was a part of her life after all.

"Here's Ellen," Dr. Monroe said. "Ellen Craig, Susan Perry."

"Hi, Susan, I'm the do-anything around here. I usually forget just what my title is, but I think it's secretary. Come on, and I'll take you to meet the others. We've set out lunch so you can take us all on in a bunch. That way, you can get the shock over. Here, just drop your things on the reception desk."

It was a small staff, and as Anne had said, with the exception of Dr. Monroe, they were all young.

There was Bill Brown, a general practitioner just out of medical school at the University of Virginia. He took her hand in a strong grip that warmed her somehow. He seemed really glad she was there.

"Welcome aboard," he said in a deep voice. "I'm glad you've come."

"He really is," Carol Evans, one of the two nurses, said. Everybody laughed.

"Not fair," Janet Parker, the other nurse, said. "Tell her why you're so glad, Bill."

"Well, I am glad," he protested.

"Sure you are," Ellen teased. "He's probably glad to meet you, Susan, but he's mostly glad because he's been doubling as a social worker. Don't listen to anything he says. We don't believe any of the wild stories he tells."

"I haven't told a single fib, not one," he said, putting Susan's hand on the back of a ladder-back chair. "Ellen's bringing you a plate from the buffet. All right?"

"Sure," she said. Already she felt relaxed with these warm people who had given up their Saturday afternoon just to make her feel at home.

"This is all of us," Janet said, "except Tim, our general handyman. He'd promised to mind the kids this afternoon for Vera, his wife, but he said to tell you he'd see you bright and early Monday or sooner than that if it turns cold."

"Cold?" The shrimp salad was good! "It's his job to fire the furnace," Dr. Monroe explained. "He and Vera are your nearest neighbors. They live in a cottage that used to be quarters for the gardener, I think. Anyhow, they're within hollerin' distance, as they say around here, so if you need them, holler."

"Seriously," Ellen said, "don't let me forget to give you their telephone number before I leave. If you need anything, do call them. They're "real people," another local expression.

"You'll have to work on your vocabulary," Bill advised, "but I'll clue you, or else you'll never get all the meanings straight."

"Remember the day right after we first opened, when we got a message from Mrs. Meadows up in Whiskey Hollow?" Ellen asked.

"I don't think any of us will ever forget it," Bill said, and Susan could sense the grin that must be on his face. "Susan, we got this message that Mrs. Meadows would like someone to carry her to the Social Services office over in the county seat. Well, we asked around and found out that Whiskey Hollow is almost inaccessible, and that the lady weighs almost two-hundred pounds."

"What did you do?" Susan asked.

"Our first reaction was "it isn't our problem," but Doc Monroe said we should accommodate the lady because records showed that she does have a heart condition. So we got busy trying to rig up a litter. Then Tim, who has lived here all his life, enlightened us. All the woman wanted was transportation. Around here, "carry" also means "take.""

And they all laughed, at themselves, Susan was sure of that.

"I'll show you your apartment now," Ellen said an hour later when the others were gathering up their things and telling her again just to let them know if she needed anything or if they were doing something all wrong.

"After all," Dr. Monroe had said, "we're not blind, and we've never been blind. There's no telling what kind of blunder we'll make. Just say so if we do."

"I'd like to see my apartment," she said in answer to Ellen's offer.

Together they walked up the curving steps and down the broad upstairs hall.

"The things you had shipped came yesterday, and Tim and Bill brought them up. If they're not where you want them, just say so, and Tim will move anything you can't."

The apartment consisted of a large sitting room with an alcove for eating, a kitchenette, a bathroom, and a bedroom that opened on a screened porch.

"The kitchen and part of your bedroom belonged to another suite of rooms," Ellen explained. "I think it's nice, especially this porch. Now, is there anything I can do before I take off?"

Susan fingered the vase of dahlias on the desk in the living room and thought of the well-stocked refrigerator in the kitchen.

"I can't think of a thing. I didn't expect all this, you know."

"We haven't done anything special," Ellen said. "We're glad you've come, and we want you to feel at home."

Home, Susan thought when the sound of Ellen's VW had faded. Home. How many meanings that word could have, and what did it mean for her? She slipped a cassette into the deck and lost herself in the music. Someday, somewhere, she would know the real meaning of the love that word brought to mind.

Suddenly she realized she had completely forgotten to telephone Eric to tell him she had arrived safely. "I'll do it in a while," she said aloud and settled back to listen and dream.

# Chapter Ten

**S**usan found that it was easy for her to fit into the work of the clinic. At first, the patients had been somewhat in awe of her; then, in the free-and-easy way of the mountain people, they often asked to see the "blind doctor" and seemed eager to tell her their problems.

"I'm not a doctor anymore," she would explain, but it did no good. If she had been doctoring before she was blind, then she was still a doctor, they said. So far as they were concerned, that was that.

"Leave them alone," Dr. Monroe advised. "You're not practicing medicine without a license or anything like that. Let them have their blind doctor."

October's days of warm, smoky sun and crisp nights held, even toward the first of November.

"It's usually cold by Halloween," Tim told her one evening when he brought over a bag of groceries Vera had picked up for her.

"I was wondering if it is always this warm this far into October," she said, handing him the money for the groceries. "If I could order weather, it would be like this."

Tim laughed. "As Mama always said, we'll pay for this later. Always happens--nice days this late in the year, and when Old Man Winter finally gets here, he breathes snow all over creation."

"Do you have much snow here?" She started to put things away.

"Do we? There are times when we don't see anybody for a week."

"Tim!"

"No, I was fooling, but sometimes we do get snowed in for a day or two. Which reminds me, Vera said to tell you that if you'd make up a list of extra things in case of bad weather, she'd be glad to get them for you. She always does that every year. Sometimes we need them, and sometimes we don't, but it never hurts to have them."

"I think that's a good idea," she said. "Do the roads get bad?"

"They're kind of slow about plowing the county roads. Of course, they've gotten better since the clinic opened, but nobody much came last winter when the weather was bad. And of course, last year was the first year the clinic was open."

"I've never been snowed in; it sounds like fun."

"Well, maybe," he said, and she could hear him putting on his jacket. "Want anything before I go?"

"No, thank you. Thank Vera for me, and tell the kids I'm going to make cookies tomorrow if they'd like to come over."

"I'll declare, Dr. Susan, you spoil the kids. It's got so they look for cookies or something like that every Saturday."

"I enjoy doing it, Tim. They're such good kids. It's ginger cookies this time, tell them."

"Will do. Good night, Dr. Susan."

"Good night, Tim, and thanks again." Before she went to bed, she stepped out to the porch. Except for a few stalwart crickets still insisting that they would live forever, the night was perfectly quiet. The moon, she knew, was full, and she stood imagining the night as she had once known it. High overhead, a bat chittered its way through its world of endless darkness, and she shivered. They had a lot in common, she and that creature of the night; only, he seemed to know where he was going.

She knew that she couldn't live forever in this little backwater of peace. Here she was important, she had a place, but someday she would have to face that big, bustling world, and fit into it with Eric.

Sometimes she felt that she had made a mistake in coming to the clinic. Was she just putting off what would come? Was she hiding from the real world?

Dr. Susan. Yes, that name said it all.

She was just playing, as Penelope had hinted. She'd been given something to do and was beginning to feel important. But it was false, as false as the title of doctor before her name.

Eric had not called for several weeks, she realized suddenly, and she felt guilty. Often days went by in which she didn't think about him. Sometimes, too, she managed to forget the old life, the old world. She would have to call and find out if Eric was sick. Surely, though, Penelope would have let her know, and she felt guilty again.

A drop of rain plopped on the clematis that grew along the porch, and she realized that the air was turning cold.

Well, they had been lucky, and she had always enjoyed the changing seasons.

Suddenly she was aware of the phone ringing in the room behind her. She rushed through the door, but just as she reached for the phone, it stopped ringing. How long, she wondered, had it been ringing before she heard it? Oh, well, if they wanted her enough, they'd call back.

When she went to close the door, she heard the rain start to come down in a torrent. The autumn days had come to an end.

Early the next morning, she was awakened by clanging and then a gurgle. At first, she wondered just what was going on, and then she knew that it must be the old coal furnace laboring into another winter's work.

It was still raining hard at three that afternoon when Sally and Bob, their hands filled with cookies, went sloshing home.

Susan felt restless for the first time since she had come to the clinic. She couldn't seem to settle down to anything.

The side door banged, and she knew it was either Vera or Tim come to check on the furnace. It boasted an automatic stoker, but Tim said he didn't trust the contraption.

She had started down the main staircase to ask whoever it was if the ball of yarn she was holding was red or green. She had had the misfortune to dump her yarn box, and all the colors were mixed together. As she reached the bottom of the steps, the bell rang.

She couldn't remember having ever heard the bell at the front door. At first, she couldn't figure out what it was, and so she just stood there.

"I'll get it, Dr. Susan," Vera said, coming up from the cellar. "Probably somebody that isn't got enough sense to know the clinic's closed. You just step in the lounge, or you'll have trouble getting away from whoever it is."

Since she was familiar with just how hard it was to get away sometimes, Susan meekly did as she was told.

She had just sat down on the love seat when she heard Vera scream.

"Vera!" she cried, rushing into the passage connected with the main hall.

She could hear a man's voice, and then what she thought was a car stopping in front of the building. What on earth?

"Dr. Susan!" Vera called. "Can you come, please? It's a child in trouble!"

"I'm on my way. Where are you?"

"In the front examining room."

"All right."

Yes, that had been a car she could hear what sounded like two people coming up the walk.

"I don't know what to do," Vera said. "All right, Vera, tell me what the situation is. I'll try to help, but if it's a real emergency, we need to call Bill or Doc."

"Susan dear," a woman's voice was calling from the front door.

For a wild moment, Susan wondered if she'd fallen down the stairs, and was suffering from concussion. The usually placid Vera was screeching that she didn't know what to do, and Susan could have sworn that she heard Penelope's voice calling her.

"What kind of emergency?" she asked. At least she sounded sane.

"A child and--" Vera began to say. "Good gracious, Susan!" the other voice interrupted. "That child is having a fit! Oh, Eric!"

Dear heaven, it was Penelope!

"The little girl's over here on the floor," Vera told Susan.

At least Vera's senses hadn't completely deserted her. Susan could have fallen over the child if Vera hadn't told her.

"All right, Vera, call Bill or Doc. I think you'll have more of a chance to find Doc, so try him first." Susan dropped to her knees.

"What kind of doctor are you?" a gruff voice said, and she could actually smell the man. "Are you afraid of her?"

"Susan!" Penelope screeched. "I tell you that the child is having a fit! Don't touch her!"

"Penelope," Susan said slowly and deliberately, "shut up."

She reached out and felt what she had expected, a small body apparently in the throes of a grand-mal seizure.

The man kneeled beside her. "I'm sorry." He spoke quietly. "What can I do to help you?"

"The cabinet over the sink--get a tongue depressor. I don't think we'll get it in now, but I'll try."

In a moment he was back, pressing the instrument into her hand. Deftly she turned the child's head to the side. "She's drenched," she said, slipping the tongue depressor between the girl's teeth. "How many seizures has she had?"

"I didn't count, but it's been going on all the way over here, about half an hour, maybe longer."

"She'll need medication. If someone doesn't get here soon, I can ask Vera to get what we need."

"I can't find either of them, Dr. Susan," Vera said from the doorway. "I left a message, though, and Mrs. Monroe is going to get Doc from wherever he is, I forget." Susan could hear the tears near the surface. Poor Vera! Probably she was picturing one of her own lying there.

"You did fine," Susan said. "It's all right. It looks worse than it is. Do you know where the keys to the medicine closet are kept?"

"Yes." Vera seemed to be regaining her composure.

"All right, go and get this." Quickly she wrote, using the pad and pen that always stayed on the shelf. She knew her writing wasn't straight.

"Can you read it?" she asked, tearing the page off and giving it to Vera.

Susan knew that no one should touch the drugs except one of the doctors or nurses, but she recognized in her patient the weak pulse and shallow breathing accompanying the dreaded status epilepticus, one seizure following another until the heart was endangered. She couldn't wait, and she was a doctor, after all.

"Yes," Vera said, and Susan could hear the relief in her voice. Someone was doing something, and she herself was helping.

"Susan, you're surely not going to give that child an injection," Penelope said incredulously a moment later.

Susan had almost forgotten about Penelope, and for a minute, she hesitated before injecting the premeasured dosage.

"Yes," she answered briefly and went on with her work.

"But, my dear, how do you know how much to give her?"

"This apparently is something of a problem in this area," Susan explained. Why was she explaining to Penelope, of all people? "Dr. Monroe told me they have several premeasured doses ready in case they have to go out on a house call."

"But, my dear, that's dangerous, and I just know you'll get into trouble being so sure of yourself."

Susan could already feel the child's thin body relaxing.

"She's already breathing better." Susan realized she'd forgotten about the man too. "She'll be all right," she told him, "but of course, Dr. Monroe can make sure. Are you her father?"

"No. I'm Dave Ward. I just happened along. I was trying to get my car out of a mud hole when her mother screamed for help. Seems the kid was looking over the fence at the pigs-- don't ask me why, please--when she had a seizure and fell over into the pen."

"Good heavens!" Susan said. Well, at least she knew what the smell was.

"I had an awful time keeping the mother pig away long enough to get her out."

"That's little Wanda Wright," Vera said. "Doc's been treating her for epilepsy, but she doesn't always take her medicine. Her mother's simple, but Wanda's a smart little thing.

"In the hog pen, you say," she went on, obviously talking to the man. "Well, I'd say you're mighty lucky. That sow of the Wrights is mighty mean."

"I'll amen that," he said.

"Did you get your car out of the mud?" Susan was beginning to be amused in spite of herself.

"No, I didn't. That's how we both got so wet. I carried her all the way."

"I heard that Percy, little Wanda's daddy, was in jail again," Vera said.

"Oh, I think I'm going to faint, Eric, I really do."

And Susan heard a plop.

"Susan, do something!" At last, Eric had found his voice. "All this is too much for Mother. You know she's frail."

Susan found herself about to giggle. "Frail"-- really, she didn't think she'd ever heard anyone, especially someone Eric's age, use that word. Penelope frail!

"All right, take it easy," she managed to say.

Where on earth was Penelope, and why didn't Eric at least tell her? Then she found the woman.

"Oops, sorry. I didn't mean to kick her. Vera, would you please--"

"Allow me," Dave said, and before Susan realized what he was going to do, he had flung a cup of water over Penelope. Penelope sputtered, no doubt sitting up.

"Eric, take Mother home," she said between little breathy sobs. "I've never seen such a place in my life. Susan darling, we'll wait for you in the car."

"I'm sorry, Penelope, what did you say?"

Her euphoria was gone, and suddenly Susan was beginning to tremble in reaction to all that had happened.

"Surely you're coming home with us. I mean, really. ..." For once, Penelope was without words.

Susan felt an arm go around her shoulders, and from the smell, she knew it was Dave.

"Sit down," he said, guiding her to a chair. "Vera, why don't you take this lady and help her get dried off a bit. Then give her a cup of tea or something. I take it she's your mother," he said, evidently addressing Eric.

"Yes, but look, I--"

"Then I suggest you take her home and put her to bed before she gets a chill."

Susan could hear Vera actually coaxing Penelope down the hall.

Everyone had momentarily forgotten about little Wanda, who sat up, and in a drugged voice said, "Penelope Pig," before promptly lying down and going back to sleep.

"Susan, I believe we need to talk," Eric said.

"Go on," Dave said. "I'll look after your patient. Should I put her on the table or something?"

"No, just throw another blanket over her and leave her where she is for now. Sure you don't mind?"

"Not a bit."

She walked with Eric to the lounge, and he closed the door.

"Eric, I'm sorry," she said, "but you should have called before you came."

"We tried last night, and when we couldn't get you, we decided to come on anyhow. Susan, please come back with us. Surely you know this isn't the place for you. These people--"

"It isn't usually like this. I'm sorry your mother was upset, but this is my world--these people are my work."

"Susan, I can't leave you here."

"You don't have the choice of leaving me or not, Eric. Look, I'll be honest with you. Penelope asked for what she got. Can't you realize that? It's too bad that she's never really grown up, but I thought you had."

She found that she was angry, angry at Penelope for her childish, patronizing ways, angry at Eric for following after his mother like a puppy, and so angry at her blindness.

"Susan," he said, and she could hear him take a deep breath, "either you come back with us now and start acting like a normal person, or--"

"Or it's over," she finished for him. Even his anger was colored by Penelope's expressions. "I think that's what you've wanted all along. You can't accept my blindness, and you don't have the guts to say so. All right, Eric, I'll do it for you."

She held out the diamond solitaire he had given her what seemed a century ago though it was only a year. "Take it. Now you can tell everyone that I've called it off."

"Susan, oh, Susan! I wish it could have been different. I wish I were different."

"But you're not, Eric. None of us can wish ourselves different. We're what we are, and change comes hard. Find someone who can share all those things you want so much. You know, I find myself wondering if we could ever have shared them. Probably if I hadn't lost my sight, something else would have come between us. We'll never know, will we?"

"Susan, I do love you," he protested.

"You probably love the me that you and I created. But right now, I don't know what the real me is. I just know I'm not the woman you want me to be, and I never could be, not now anyhow."

She could hear Dr. Monroe's voice in the hall. At least the responsibility of Wanda was off her shoulders.

"Are you sure, Susan?" Eric said, and as she heard the pleading warmth in his voice, she felt the old magic for a moment.

"Yes, Eric, I'm sure. Now you'd better get started. You have a long drive ahead of you, and the weather report calls for sleet later on this evening."

She slipped her arm through his in the old way, and together, but separated forever, they walked toward the front hall.

# Chapter Eleven

"**G**ood-bye, Eric," Susan said as they reached the main hall.

"Susan--"

"No, Eric," she said. "There's really nothing else for us to talk about. I hear Vera coming with Penelope. You'd better get going--it's getting late."

She knew she'd had enough, at least for a while. There was no way she could make polite conversation with anyone. She turned and went quickly up the stairs.

Her living room was blessedly quiet and warm. She stood beside the hissing radiator and realized how cold she was.

There was nothing for her to do. Vera and Doc were in charge now, and Penelope and Eric would be almost to the main highway. No one could make demands on her person or her time. She burst into tears.

"All right," she told herself ten minutes later as she started to run a hot bath. "The old life is really over and gone. Now, what are you going to do?"

The immediate answer was obvious, and so she discarded her clothes, which smelled suspiciously like a pig, and lowered herself into the warm water.

She had just put on jeans and a bulky sweater when someone knocked on her door. She wanted to ignore the knock, but there was no way anyone would think she was out, so she crossed the living room and opened the door.

"You all right, Susan?" Dr. Monroe asked.

"Sure. I thought I'd better clean up before you sent me out to the pen."

"Come down and have coffee. Vera brought over some sandwiches too. Everyone's gone except for Wanda, and she's still asleep. Even Vera's gone home to feed her brood."

She couldn't think of anything she wanted to do less, but it would be rude to refuse.

He slipped his arm through hers. "You did a good job this afternoon," he said when they had settled in the lounge with coffee and the plate of sandwiches.

"Come on, Doc, I didn't do anything that Vera couldn't have done. I knew what the medication should be, and anyone could have given it. I'm really not sure that I should have done it."

"You were certainly at the right place at the right time, and of course, you should have given the medication. You'd finished medical school, and lacked only a few weeks of finishing your residency."

"I should have waited a little longer, but I didn't like the way her heart was acting," she admitted, warming to his praise, although she knew that what she had done was nothing.

"I know," he said, putting another sandwich on her plate. "I've been faced with the same situation. I'm going to run some tests. There may be a weakness there."

"Vera told me that you'd been treating her for epilepsy, but that she didn't always take her medication."

"It always amazes me what Vera knows, but she's right. Wanda's a bright little thing, but her mother's retarded. The epilepsy's the result of a fall during infancy they say. I don't know; I suspect it's more like a blow on the head, but who can tell?"

"Vera says Wanda's father is in jail. Can't Social Services do anything?"

"It's hard to say what's best to do. It's the old question of whether she'd be better off shunted from foster home to foster home, or whether it's better to let her take her chances with her parents. We can't exactly prove that they're unfit, but I'm not going to let her go home for a few days."

"I'm glad," she said, "but what are you going to do with her?"

"I've sent Tim over to tell her that she'll be staying with him and Vera for a few days. They help out in cases like this, whenever they're needed. Vera said she'd be glad to have her. I'd have sent the mother a note, but I don't think the woman can read."

"Let Wanda stay with me."

Susan was shocked at the request. What made her make such an offer?

"Are you sure?" He got up, and she could hear him knocking out his pipe.

"Yes. That is if you think it'll be all right. Vera has so much to do, and, honestly, to say that their house is noisy is putting it mildly. Those little monkeys are darling, but you'll have to admit they're full of life."

"You're right--that is putting it mildly, but I don't want to take your free time, Susan."

"What would I do with it?" she asked. "I'm not going anywhere, and it would be easier for her to rest here with me. Isn't that bedroom next to my apartment still furnished?"

"Yes," he said, "we left it in case we'd need it in bad weather. I'll get Vera to check the bed and the bathroom. What about food?"

"Do you mean, do I have enough, or do you mean can I manage? The answer's yes on both counts. Honestly, Doc, I'll enjoy having her."

"Sorry, but I told you when you first came that I'd ask stupid things. I won't pretend that this won't be a help. I hated to ask Vera to take it on, especially since we can't be absolutely sure that Wanda won't have another seizure. I'll feel better about her if she's with you. We'd take her, but Edna's youngest is with us for the weekend and has been exposed to chickenpox. I'd rather not risk that on top of Wanda's other troubles right now. I checked her file, and she hasn't had it."

"Then it's settled. You can schedule whatever tests you want to be done for the first of the week, and we can get it all over at the same time."

They sat listening to the rain and the ticking of a mantel clock, which had been part of the original furnishings of the old house.

"Susan, working for us hasn't caused--well, any personal problems for you, has it?"

She heard him return his cup to the tray on the coffee table.

"No. I sometimes get the feeling that my whole life is a problem," she said finally.

"I'm not trying to pry into what's none of my business, you know that."

"I know."

"It was pretty obvious, though, that things weren't exactly going well for you. Can I help in any way? I was concerned when you first took the job because you'd be stuck way out here with no means of independent transportation. You know, we can probably find a place for you in Windburg, and we could take turns seeing that you get to work. We'd work out something. Just say the word. That would give you a little more freedom of movement."

"I wish it were that simple."

"Is there anything that would help, anything that I, or any of the others for that matter, can do?"

"At the risk of sounding self-pitying," she said, "there's nothing, unless you can help me regain my sight."

She hated herself the minute the words were out, but there was no way of taking them back.

"I wish I could," he said, speaking softly, "but--and this sounds preachy--you know there are a lot of people walking around with 20/20 who can't see as much as you see. You've done a fantastic job here, Susan, and I'm not just saying that. If you'll pardon my phrasing, you've seen right through to the inner being of these people. They love you and more importantly, they respect you."

"I'm glad," she said, and she knew that she meant it. "I shouldn't have said that, about my sight, I mean, but sometimes. ..."

"I'm probably way out of line, but I have to say this. You're too good to have to be hurt by that woman who was here today. I think she'd cause trouble for any woman who dared to lay hands on her darling boy. Oh, I think she'd tolerate someone she could control, but you've got too much on the ball to be controlled by her or anyone else. You're your own person, whether you know it or not."

"Thank you, but the question has been settled." She showed him the hand that had worn the diamond.

He took it and held it for a minute. "Want to know the truth?"

"Yes," she said.

"I'm glad this has happened. You're too good for them, both of them. Now, let's you and me go see what Miss Wanda's room looks like. There's linen down here, and we'll get the bed ready."

Fifteen minutes later, they found Wanda starting to wake up.

"Hi there, pretty girl," Dr. Monroe said. "How are you doing?"

"All right, I guess. Is it morning?"

"No, but it'll soon be suppertime, and I've got a surprise for you. You're going to stay here with us at the clinic for a few days. Vera might even take you for a trip over to Charlottesville to have a few tests, but we'll see."

"Really?" Wanda exclaimed, and Susan heard her throw her feet over the side of the table.

"Don't get too frisky," Dr. Monroe said, lowering the rail. "This is Dr. Susan. She helped you when Mr. Ward brought you here. Do you remember anything about it?"

"I was looking at Penelope,"--so the pig's name really was Penelope--"and I guess I got sick. I'm sorry I forgot my pills again."

"Well, you'll remember from now on, won't you?" Susan said, putting her arm around her.

"You're going to stay here with Dr. Susan. We've fixed a bed for you right next to her room, and you'll have a bathroom all your own."

"What color?"

"Green, I think, but you'll see." He helped her off the table.

"I'm really going to stay? I'm not going home?"

"Not right away. Now, meet Dr. Susan." Susan held out her hand, and the little hand was placed in it.

"Wanda," she said, "do you know that I'm blind? You see with your eyes, but I see with my fingers and my nose and my ears."

"You got the teacher to give Peggy a seat in the front row 'cause she didn't always hear things. I know about you. Peggy says you're like special. You bought her a hamburger when they tested to see how good she could hear."

"That's right. When they finished the tests, we went down the street and had lunch."

"Peggy said she was your eyes crossing the street. Will I be your eyes?"

"Sure. Come on. I think the first thing we'd better do is get you in the tub and get your hair washed."

"Where are my shoes?"

"Vera took them and your clothes to get them clean," Dr. Monroe said. "The floors are nice and warm. You can run upstairs in the hospital gown you have on, without your shoes."

"We'll find something for you to put on," Susan promised, taking her hand. "It'll be all right just between us girls. Come on, or you might get cold."

"Sure you don't need some help?" Susan said as she turned off the water.

"No, I'm almost nine, you know. I can take my bath by myself, but thank you for helping me with my hair."

"You're welcome, honey," Susan said, wondering where Wanda had come by her proper little way of talking. "I'll go get one of my robes. You'll have to hold it up when you walk, but you'll be careful, won't you?"

"Oh, yes," she said, splashing. "Can I really put on your robe?"

"Sure. Sorry, I don't have any slippers to fit you, but the floors are carpeted and nice and warm. I expect Tim will bring some of your things back, but you can still wear my robe if you'd like."

"I wear my sister's things sometimes."

"I didn't know you had a big sister," Susan said, sitting on the edge of the tub.

"Her name's Jenny, but she's gone."

"I'm sorry. You must miss her," Susan said.

"I didn't get to see her much, just when I went to visit her at Mama Ross's house. She lived with Mama Ross. They educated her."

"I see. Where has she gone?"

"I don't know. She went away with Buddy, and they ain't-- they haven't heard from them for over a year."

Susan began to feel that she was in over her head. Maybe she'd better change the subject, and let Doc or the all-knowing Vera straightens it out for her.

"Okay," she said as she stood up, "I'm going to fix supper. Hamburgers and fries, okay?"

"Are they! My most very favorites. We don't have them at home, but when I go to see Mama Ross, I always have them."

"Well, you're going to have them tonight, so get going with that bath," Susan said, playfully splashing water over the child's thin back.

"I didn't know there was an older sister," Susan said later that night when Vera came in to check on the furnace.

Wanda was sound asleep, with the covers tucked up around her chin.

"Now, that's a story," Vera said. "Let's sit down here in the examining room, where you can hear her if she calls but where she can't hear us. She's a proud little thing, you know."

"I know," Susan said, perching on a stool. "Jenny is really her half-sister. Old Percy was married once before; of course, that was before his drinking completely took over his life. Pretty girl she was, came from a good family. She died when Jenny was born. Some of us think that was what really started Percy's drinking real bad. It's like a disease with him."

"Has he ever gotten help?" the social worker in Susan asked.

"He's been away who knows how many times. Now he just doesn't care. Jenny's--well, let me see--she must be almost twenty. Sarah Ross was her mother's friend, and she took little Jenny to raise with her own boy, Buddy. They grew up together, but you could see how it was with them."

"What do you mean?" Susan asked.

"They loved each other from the time they were old enough to feel that kind of love. It didn't do a bit of good: Sarah ranting and begging; and Ezra, her husband, threatening. Jenny and Buddy loved each other, and that was that."

"But what was the objection? They weren't related."

"I couldn't exactly understand that either, but they were brought up together, you see, and somehow for Sarah and Ezra, it didn't seem right. They said it was like brother and sister. Oh, you know folks around here have funny ways."

Susan smiled in spite of herself. She knew that Vera's family had moved there when she was three, but she was still an outsider, accepted because of Tim, who belonged.

"I guess we all have funny ideas about something, Vera, but go on."

"Anyhow, last year they just up and run away. Nobody's heard one word from them since."

"Wanda said she used to visit them." "The Rosses have always taken an interest in little Wanda. They kept her a lot in the summer so the girls could get to know each other. Did you see how proper she talks? Well, that was from Jenny. Can't say that Sarah and Ezra have much education, but they saw to it that Buddy and Jenny got their schooling. Jenny worked a lot with Wanda. It's a shame things turned out the way they did."

"Does Wanda still visit Mr. and Mrs. Ross?"

"For some reason, her mama's taken against them--jealousy, I expect. Anyhow, she fusses about her going there to visit, so she doesn't go as much as she did once."

"Thank you for telling me this, Vera," Susan said as she got off her stool. "I want to help that little girl, and maybe I can talk to Mrs. Ross. For starters, I think she needs some better clothes."

"You can say that three times," Vera agreed. "Her mother sent over the most awful-looking things you've ever seen. My sister's little girl is a little bigger than Wanda, and I sent Tim over there after supper to get some of her things she'd outgrown. I'll bring them over in the morning, and we'll try them on. Mercy, look at the time! Tim will think I ran off or something. Need anything before I go?"

When Susan had locked the side door behind Vera, she stood listening to the familiar night sounds of the clinic.

Somewhere she heard it, the old saying, "Home is what you make it." Well, she mused, as she started up the stairs, surely it was where you found it, and she went to check on Wanda before going to bed.

# Chapter Twelve

The next day, Sunday, was bright and clear. A playful wind toyed with the leaves, blowing them in first one direction and then another.

Vera came in just as Susan and Wanda were finishing breakfast. Susan was amazed at how many clothes her sister's girl had "outgrown," and she suspected that the sister had sacrificed some of them.

"You'll go home looking like a film star coming back from location," Susan told Wanda as they hung the garments in the closet. "Thank you for telling me what color they are."

"Oh, you're welcome. I said I'd be your eyes, didn't I?"

"Yes, you did, and you're doing a great job. It's too late for us to go to Sunday school, so what would you like to do?"

"If you don't mind, I'd like to listen to your record player."

"The stereo, of course. We can listen to the radio, records, or tapes. Come on, and I'll show you how to use it."

Right after lunch, Vera came in to say that her sister and her children had dropped in, and they would like Wanda to come over to play.

"They're staying for supper, Dr. Susan, and I'd be glad to have you and Wanda both."

"Thank you, Vera, but I have a few things that I really should get done here. I know Wanda would love to come, though, wouldn't you?"

"Yes, please," she said, getting off the floor where she had been arranging the tapes in alphabetical order.

"Don't forget your pill when you've finished eating," Susan reminded her.

"Oh, I won't let her forget," Vera assured her. "Get your jacket, honey. It's cool out there. We'd love to have you, Dr. Susan, but I understand. Come on, Wanda, I have your pill."

Susan was surprised at how empty the apartment felt when Wanda had gone. She'd really have to be careful, or she'd miss her when she went home.

When the phone rang, she started not to answer it. She couldn't take another confrontation with Eric. Only the thought that there might be something wrong at Vera's made her cross the room and lift the receiver.

"Dr. Perry, this is Dave Ward."

For a minute, she felt confused. She had been so sure that it would be Vera. Dave Ward?

"Oh, yes, Mr. Ward." Now she remembered; he had brought Wanda to the clinic.

"I'm not interrupting anything, am I?"

"No, of course not. How are you? You didn't catch cold splashing around in all that rain, did you?"

"No, I'm a hardy soul. How's your little patient?"

"Doing fine, thanks. She's over playing at Vera's. Doc decided that we'd better keep an eye on her for a few days, so she's staying with me. I'm sorry I didn't get a chance to thank you yesterday for bringing her all that way."

"I was just glad I was there."

"It had to be tedious, to say the least," she said, settling on the sofa. "I mean, she couldn't have been easy to manage in her condition."

"Oh, I just stopped when I needed to, but I'll tell the truth: I was glad to get there and to find someone in. I'd forgotten it was Saturday."

"As you know now, I live upstairs at the clinic."

"Look, I owe you an apology," he said, the words coming out in a rush, "and I'd like to take you out to dinner to make it."

"Why on earth do you think you owe me an apology?"

"I was pretty rude at first, but I didn't realize you were blind. I thought you were just hesitating because the kid was dirty and wet, and that fool of a woman kept screeching."

"Don't think anything about it. People often don't realize it when they first meet me. I'm told that I don't look blind. I can understand how you felt."

"Anyhow, will you come out with me?"

"Look," she said, beginning to get impatient, "I've already said it's all right. You don't have to do anything to make it up. I'm not a little girl, you know."

"You sure make it hard for a fella, as they say around here. I don't think I have to ask you. Has it ever occurred to you that if an apology was all I had on my mind, I'd have sent you flowers?"

"Okay, then, what do you have on your mind?"

"I just think I'd like to get to know you better, that's all. Listen, I started all wrong. Let's start again. You've just answered the phone. ... Dr. Perry, this is David Ward. We met yesterday, and I'd like to take you out to dinner if you're not busy. Is that better?"

Susan found herself laughing. "Look, I'd like to come, but there's Wanda."

"You just said she's over with Mother Vera. Call and tell her we're going out. I promise I've taken a bath. Honest, I don't smell a bit like a pig."

"All right. Where are we going? I mean, how should I dress?"

"Are you kidding? You've been here long enough to know there are few really formal places around. I'm coming the way I am, pretty casual. Pick you up in an hour?"

"Sure," she said.

"Okay, see you then."

She told herself she was foolish, but she felt excited. After all, this would be the first real date she had had since she had lost her sight.

Of course, there had been plays and concerts when she had been at the rehab center, but that had certainly not been a date. And with surprise, she realized that Eric had never taken her out after she lost her sight.

"You're acting like a girl on her first date," she said aloud.

In a way it was. Hadn't she told herself just the day before that her old life was over? Well, when something ends, something new usually starts.

As she picked up her bag and went to the living room to wait for Dave, she reminded herself that she was making too much of a casual date. No matter what he said, he was probably just asking her by way of apology for his brusque behavior the day before.

The bell downstairs rang, and she went slowly to answer it. After all, she didn't have to let him know it was her first blind date, and she giggled to herself at the pun.

"Hi," she said, opening the door. "Ready?" he asked.

For an answer, she smiled and closed and checked the door.

"I might as well tell you from the beginning that I know less about blindness than I do epilepsy," he said, "and that's not much. I did learn a little about seizures in a first-aid course, but I'll probably go off and leave you standing someplace."

"Don't worry about that." She took his arm. "I yell real loud. And, just in case, I carry a folding cane in my bag. Just keep walking along the way you're doing now. That's fine."

He was probably almost six feet tall, she decided. His arm felt strong and muscular under her hand, and he walked with the stride of one who knows exactly where he's going.

"My car's a VW Rabbit," he said, opening the door.

"Maybe not elegant," she said as she ducked the necessary distance and slid in, "but handy, to say the least, on these roads. Incidentally, when did you get it unstuck?"

"Late yesterday. I called Ezra Ross, and he came with his trusty tractor."

"Ezra Ross--that's Wanda's friend." "They were upset about what had happened. She was going to call Doc. That's a sad situation. Did anyone tell you about it?"

"Vera did last night."

"Oh, yes, I had forgotten about Vera. She's the greatest, and if you want to know anything about anybody around here, just ask her. The difference between Vera and most people who know everything is that she really does, and doesn't tell it unless she sees a good reason to."

"Are you from around here?" she asked as they turned right onto the main highway.

"My father taught at the high school in Windburg. I was born here, but he took a job in Arlington when I was ten. I moved back here--to Windburg that is--about a year ago."

"To teach?"

"No. I'm the editor and owner of the Windburg News. Dad died two years ago, and I inherited a little money. When I heard the paper was for sale, I borrowed the rest, and here I am."

"Have you always been in journalism?"

"I was with the Washington Post in a very menial position. I think that inside every big-city journalist there lurks a small-town reporter. I just happened to have the means to let mine out."

"And the courage too," she said. "It must be a big change."

"Yes," he admitted, "but most days I go home feeling it's worth all the headaches. Here we are. Sorry, I forgot you can't tell where "here" is."

"As a matter of fact, I think I can. I smell seafood. It's the Red Lobster, right?"

"Right, but considering it's the only seafood place around, that didn't take much detection on your part."

She took his arm, and he pulled her a bit closer as they moved into the restaurant.

"Do you mean you aren't going to tell me just how wonderful I was to figure that out?" she said, smiling as he took her coat and put her hand on the back of her chair.

"No way, woman, do you get a compliment out of me until you deserve one. Seriously, do people really do that?"

"You'd be surprised at the things people do. Sometimes I feel so much like a phony. I mean, when is a compliment because I'm a great person, and when is it because I'm "great for a blind person"?"

"Yeah, I see what you mean, but we all have that problem to one extent or another. So few people in our modern world ever say just what they mean. We're forced by our society to go on and on about things that don't mean a thing."

"You know," she said, "I think that's one reason I like this area so much. The people usually say just what they mean, and if you don't happen to like it--well, that's your hard luck."

He laughed. Not a forced strangled laugh, but a good deep one. "That just about says it all. Hey, here's the menu. Want me to read it, or do you know what you want?"

She remembered that she hadn't gone through her usual plan about what to order, and for a minute, she felt afraid. What if she made a mess?

"You order first, while I'm thinking," she said, stalling for time.

"I'd like the lobster," he said, and she could hear a grin in his voice, "but it's the first time out with this girl, and I don't want her to think I'm a pig. Oh, I didn't know how that would come out." Suddenly they were both laughing, to the surprise of the waitress.

"Sorry," he said, "it's a private joke. How about the combination plate? Have you decided yet, Sue?"

"The same, I think," she said, and she didn't even stop to wonder just what was on the plate. She'd handle it when it came.

"Would you like to come in for coffee?" she asked later when he had unlocked the main door of the clinic and handed her keys back to her.

The October night had fallen, and a cold wind blew through the branches of the pine trees along the drive. She felt sad. It had been a fun evening, and she found that she was reluctant to let go of it. She knew she was in the grip of a superstitious fear that once the day was gone, she might never find another like it again.

"I really shouldn't," he said, but he came in and closed the door. "Shouldn't you be collecting your little charge, and putting her to bed?"

She touched the hands of her Braille watch. "Not quite yet. It's only a little after eight. Vera will bring her over. She'll see my lights. Come on up for a while if you'd like to."

"Okay, but I really don't care for coffee. Hey, I like your place. I can remember when this was a private home. I was never inside, though."

He flung himself on the sofa and caught her hand. "Thanks, Sue. I had fun. We'll do it again if you say the word."

"I'm the one who should be saying thanks," she said, sitting beside him. He didn't let her hand go.

"Look," he said, "I'm not known for my tact. Is it really all right if we do it again? I mean, well, that guy yesterday. ... This sounds old-fashioned, but--"

"Am I spoken for?" she asked, and she smiled. "No, not anymore." She held out her left hand. "See, all empty."

"I saw a ring there yesterday," he confessed. "I kept wondering all through dinner where it was. I mean, you might have just forgotten to put it on after you did the breakfast dishes."

Now he was holding both her hands. The warm strength of his touch felt good, and she reminded herself that it meant nothing. He was probably just being kind to her.

"I should say I'm sorry, but I can't." He let go of her left hand but went on holding the right. "Then, can we do it again? Dinner, I mean."

"I suppose so," she said.

"Well, guess I'd better be going."

He stood and pulled her with him. "No," she said as he pulled her toward him.

"Sorry," he said. "I told you I don't know the meaning of the word tact. I'll call you and thanks again."

"I hear Wanda coming now," she said and found that she felt both relief and disappointment.

"Hi," she said, as Wanda seemed to blow through the door. "Do you two know each other?"

"Sure," Wanda said. "I met him at Mama Ross's house. Thanks for bringing me to Dr. Susan's yesterday."

"You're welcome," he said seriously, as though to someone his own age. "Glad I could do it."

"Did you have fun?" Susan asked.

"Oh, sure. But I'm glad to be back with you. Can I have something to eat before I go to bed?"

"That depends on what you have in mind."

"Well. ..."

"Crackers and milk, that's all," Susan said, deciding for her. "Go and help yourself."

"Okay. Would you care for some too, Dave?" she asked, taking one of her flights into young ladyhood.

"No, thank you, I'm on my way.

You and Dr. Susan take good care of each other."

"Sure, I love Dr. Susan. She took good care of me yesterday, didn't she?"

"She did a wonderful job--very professional, I'd say. No, Sue, don't come down, unless you have to lock up."

"It'll lock by itself," she said. "Okay. I'll call you."

It wasn't until she had kissed Wanda good night and gone back to the living room that she remembered his half-kidding words: "No way, woman, will I compliment you until you deserve it." Had he really thought she handled the situation yesterday in a professional way? And she actually blushed at how silly she was being.

Exactly like a girl on her first date, she told herself again, and she turned off the light.

# Chapter Thirteen

It seemed to Susan that the next few weeks flew by on wings of work. With the coming of winter, patients seemed to come out of the very side of the mountain: the old and the sick, all linked by that one common denominator, poverty.

"Where are they all coming from?" she asked, almost in desperation at the end of an especially busy afternoon.

"It happens every year," Janet told her. "I was Dr. Wilson's nurse, you know, and every year around this time, we'd brace ourselves. I guess the cold weather must take its toll on bodies already weakened by time or hard work. For so many of them, there's never quite enough to eat, or at least not the right things. It'll go on like this for a month or two, then settle down again."

"It's this way in the cities too, except that it usually happens a little later there. I just hadn't thought too much about it before."

"How's the new member of your family?" Janet asked, starting to sterilize the last of the instruments for the day.

"She's fine," Susan said. "You know, I'll have to admit that I'm glad to have her. She's no trouble, and, as she's proud of saying, she's my eyes."

"Can you imagine her mother just going off like that?"

Janet said as she closed the sterilizer with a bang. "Vera said that when she took Wanda home that day, it was almost creepy."

"I expect it was," Susan agreed. "You know she even left the cat wandering around looking for food. Vera has it."

Wanda had gone to take tests on Monday after she had come to stay with Susan. It had been agreed that Vera would take her home when they got back from Charlottesville.

"I wish I could stay," she had said, clinging to Susan that morning.

"I know, but your mother must miss you. Now, go on like a good girl. I'll come to see you, and you can spend the weekend with me often, I promise."

But late that afternoon, Vera had come back with Wanda and her things.

"I didn't know what else to do," she had said. "Wanda's mother has taken all her things. There's no doubt in my mind that she's gone for good. Do you want me to take Wanda with me? She won't be a speck of trouble."

Susan hadn't wanted Vera to take Wanda, and Doc had agreed.

"She's happy with you, and if you don't mind, it's a solution until the authorities can decide just what's to be done with her. Percy's in jail for six months this time, and something will have to be done. You know as well as I do, though, how scarce good foster homes are, especially around here."

"I want her to stay with me for as long as necessary. If there's any question of extra money for her room--"

"We have so much use for that room," he said, and Susan could hear the smile in his voice. "Don't be silly, Susan--the room's been just sitting there. I'll bring the situation up before the board, of course, but there's no problem if you're sure. Vera would be glad to have her, but this seems the best plan."

Now it was the middle of December, and as Susan said good night to Janet and started up the stairs, she realized Christmas was only a few days away. She would have to get busy. She smiled, thinking how Wanda counted off the days until Christmas Eve every morning before she left for school.

"What do you want for Christmas?" Susan had asked her one morning.

"Want? Oh, nothing. I just want Christmas Eve to come, that's all."

Susan, wondering if Wanda had ever had a real Christmas, had determined to go all out with this year's celebration.

If you don't get busy, it'll be New Year's Day, she told herself as she reached the top of the stairs.

"Dr. Susan," Wanda called from the living room. "Dave's on the phone."

"Thank you. Now go get started on your homework. Miss Ingleman said your spelling needs some extra work. I have a Braille list of your words, and I'll be there to call them out in a few minutes." She picked up the receiver, giving the child's bottom a little swat.

"Hi. I called to see if you'd like to go out for dinner, and maybe do some Christmas shopping," Dave said.

"I'd love to, but I really shouldn't leave Wanda."

"We've fixed that up already. I called Vera, and Wanda's invited to have dinner with them. I thought we'd go over to Charlottesville. We might as well get knocked down along with about a dozen other shoppers. Honest, Sue, I was over there last week, and you have to fight for your life."

"Silly. Okay. I'll go over her spelling lesson, and I'll be ready. Fancy dress?"

"No way, woman. Remember to put on your running shoes. I tell you that place is dangerous."

She smiled fifteen minutes later as she put the finishing touches on her makeup. Since that first evening, she and Dave had fallen into the comfortable habit of having dinner together at least once a week. She knew she'd miss those evenings if they were to stop, but every time he left her at her door, she cringed in fear that he would expect something she knew she wasn't ready to give. Not since that first time, though, had he even tried to kiss her. His good night was a warm pressure on her hand.

She told herself over and over again that that was all she wanted. She wasn't ready for the complication of her own feelings, much less those of another. He was a friend, nothing more, she reminded herself as she answered the door later. They were both lonely; that was all.

"You look pretty," he said as he held her coat for her.

"Thank you. Wanda says this is her most very favorite dress," she told him, and they both laughed.

"Is she at Vera's?"

"She went over with Tim when he came to do something or other to the furnace."

"Then we're off," he said, giving her his arm. "Do you realize how close Christmas is?" she asked later after they had stored the last of their packages in the trunk of the car and settled in for the ride home.

"I'm afraid I do. Is Wanda excited?"

"You know, that's sort of strange. She counts off the days until Christmas Eve, but she doesn't seem excited at all in the usual way. It's like she wants Christmas Eve to come, but doesn't really care about Christmas itself."

"Kids are funny," he said. "Probably she's really never had a real Christmas, and she's afraid to let herself even think about anything beyond the day before. Who knows?"

"I suppose that's it. I've tried to work up some enthusiasm on her part, but it doesn't seem to make any difference."

"Is Santa Claus coming?"

"Oh, no. She told me she'd pretend for Vera's kids because they're little, but she just didn't believe that stuff."

"At least we won't have to stay up half the night to put out presents, then."

"We?" she asked.

"I hadn't exactly gotten around to asking, but could we--all three of us, I mean--spend Christmas Eve together? I'll treat you, girls, to dinner wherever you say."

"Better still," she suggested, "why don't we girls fix dinner for you? You've never had dinner with me at the apartment. Honestly, I won't poison you. I'm a pretty good cook for a blind woman."

"Don't, Sue," he said, and he laid his hand over hers where it rested on her lap. "Don't always make fun of yourself. I'm sure you're a good cook, period. I don't judge you by your blindness; you know that."

"Doesn't everyone, when it comes down to it?" she couldn't help saying. "It's there, Dave, and people can't forget it. Sometimes I think that I'm good but not quite good enough, as a person, I mean."

"You've got to believe me when I say that you think about yourself as blind more than I do. Sure, there are people who will always put it there as a barrier between them and you, but I don't, and I'm getting tired of your doing it. You're blind and we can't change that, no matter how much we'd like to. That's where it ends for me."

"I wish I could believe that, but I can't. I'm not normal, not really."

"Who is normal?"

The car stopped, and she realized that they were back at the clinic.

"You know what I mean," she said as she reached for her door handle.

"Yes, I know what you mean, but do you know what I mean?" He caught her hand and held it. "You don't want to admit, not even to yourself, that I might see you, the real you. You know what I think? I think you're afraid."

"What would I be afraid of?" she asked defensively, and she heard the anger in his voice echoed in her own. This was the first time she had seen him even ruffled since that first day at the clinic.

"You're afraid of yourself," he told her, and his grip on her hand became hard. "I can understand it, Sue, but it's not fair to those of us who--who love you."

He had spoken the last two words so softly that she almost couldn't hear them.

"No," she said, pulling away. "No, don't say that. You don't love me. Maybe you think you do, but you love the picture of the blind woman depending on you for everything. I think men need something like that."

"That's not fair. I've never given you any reason to feel that way. I know you won't admit it, but that louse hurt you. I'll tell you something else. You don't want to see"--and he stressed the word see--"that he hurt your pride more than he actually hurt you. He stripped you down to the bone of your pride and left you there in the cold to hurt. I won't do that to you. Give me a chance to show you that I won't."

He caught her to him then and kissed her hard, insistently.

"There," he said, releasing her. "That's the first installment. I love you, and I don't give up easily. I'm going to show you, in spite of yourself, that there's only love between us. To me, love is the greatest equalizer in the world. You've faced and conquered so many things, Sue. Please meet and conquer yourself. If you don't, someday circumstances are going to force you to face yourself and life, whether you think you're ready or not."

"Don't spoil things, Dave. It's been such fun being together and sharing things. Don't you see, now it won't be the same? Why can't you just let it be?" She knew that the tears that had betrayed her so many times were threatening again.

"I'm sorry, but I can't," Dave answered. He got out to hold the door for her.

"I won't come in with you," he said when he'd unlocked the main door. "I'm sorry if anything I've done or said has hurt you. I have a bad habit of saying what's on my mind, or in my heart. Forgive me."

Before she could answer, he had gone.

After she had told Wanda good night and turned out the lights, Susan sat for a long time thinking. She just wasn't ready for an involvement of any kind. If she had given Dave the wrong impression, she was sorry. She had enjoyed his company, and certainly, she felt comfortable with him. But she didn't love him, she told herself.

She felt that she couldn't, shouldn't love anyone. Her emotions were too tangled and had been for a long time, even before she lost her sight.

This last thought came as a surprise, but she knew it was the truth. Her childhood had been a lonely one, filled with a sense of duty imposed on her by parents who had no idea of the inner needs and longings of a child.

She knew that in their own way, they had loved her very much, but she understood now that they had probably been somewhat in awe of the child nature had thrust on them in later years. She had never really belonged in that house of polished floors and quiet music.

Now she wondered if she would ever belong anywhere, to anyone. She had falsely believed that she belonged to Eric, to his world of dreams and ambition. She had been right when she had told him that something else, if not her blindness, would eventually have come between them.

Only her work had opened a place for her, and now that also was gone. True, she had her work here at the clinic, but was that, too, unreal? Would she ever be able to reach out without self-consciousness, without fear, and grasp life? No, not now that she was blind. That had added the final fear to her life.

"Dr. Susan," Wanda called from her room. "Do you think it'll snow Christmas Eve?"

"I don't know, but the long-range forecast is calling for it. Won't it be fun to have a white Christmas?"

"Do they know what they're talking about?" Wanda asked, and Susan heard what sounded like worry in her voice.

"Sometimes they do, and sometimes they don't. Why? Don't you want a white Christmas?"

"No, I don't," Wanda told her, and the words were emphatic. "Please pray it won't snow. Please, Dr. Susan."

Later, Susan was to remember the childish plea; but now, filled with her own pleading for peace, she paid almost no attention.

"All right. Now get to sleep. Tomorrow's the last day of school before the Christmas vacation and you have your party, remember. You don't want to be too tired to enjoy it."

"But God won't let it snow for Christmas, will He, Dr. Susan?"

"Honey, God does whatever's best. Now go to sleep, you little monkey."

"Dr. Susan."

"Yes, Wanda?"

"I love you."

Susan crossed her bedroom and went into Wanda's room.

"I love you too," she said, hugging Wanda's warm, flannel-clad body. "Now you stop fooling around and go to sleep."

"Okay. Remember about praying there's no snow."

"Go to sleep," Susan said as she pulled up the covers.

"Dr. Susan, do you have any nieces or nephews? Babies, I mean."

"No. I don't have any sisters or brothers."

"No sisters?"

"None. Why?"

"Oh, I was just wondering about babies, you know."

Oh, no! Dear Lord, Susan was actually praying; please let's not have a birds-and-bees conversation, not tonight.

"Come on. I heard the clock strike ten, and that's way past your bedtime. I'm going to bed, and you get to sleep. Stop worrying about the snow. I haven't known a long-range forecast to be right in ages. Okay?"

"Okay. Good night."

And again, Susan didn't stop to wonder why Wanda had so many questions.

# Chapter Fourteen

Almost everyone over sixty who came to the clinic those last few days before Christmas Eve predicted it. The cattle huddled close in the fields spoke of snow in their plaintive voices. The cold wind blowing down from the mountain added its voice, but the weather bureau disagreed.

On the twenty-third, the earlier forecast of snow changed, and a Christmas more suited to Florida than to Virginia was predicted.

Wanda went around singing about babies and wise men until Susan thought she'd scream. Maybe she would be glad when they found a home for Wanda, she thought, and immediately she was so sorry that she gave the little girl a hug.

"Are you really looking forward to Christmas?" Susan asked.

"I guess so, but it's tomorrow I want to come. Oh, it's almost Christmas Eve," Wanda sang, and she went skipping down the stairs to bring in the mail for Ellen.

Susan couldn't help smiling when she thought about how seriously Wanda took that little job. They were the last on the rural-delivery schedule so that it was always after school when the little jeep pulled up at the box at the end of the drive.

"I'll bring in the mail for you, Miss Ellen," she had said the first week she'd been with Susan. "I'd like to, please."

Ellen had told Susan that she hadn't missed a single day.

"I do love you, Dr. Susan," Wanda said as she came skipping back to Susan's living room. She fairly threw herself into her arms.

"I love you too, but what brought all that on?" Susan asked, releasing herself. "You get busy straightening your room. I'm going to straighten mine. I don't have any more appointments until the day after Christmas, so I need to get some things done around here. Get going."

There hadn't been a word from Dave since he had left her at the door a week earlier. Of course, that was the way she wanted it, she told herself, but still. ...

The snow began to fall in the night. When they got up on Christmas Eve morning, over six inches had piled up and it was snowing hard.

"So much for forecasts," Susan said as she set Wanda's oatmeal in front of her. "Something wrong, honey?" she added, sitting down on her side of the little round table. "You've hardly said a word since you got up. Are you feeling all right?"

"I guess so. I mean, I'm not sick. I remembered my medicine and everything."

"I know you did." Susan picked up her spoon. "I thought you couldn't wait until Christmas Eve."

"Do you think the roads will be all right?"

"I don't really know," Susan said part of her mind on finishing a sweater she was knitting for Wanda's Christmas present. Wanda had coveted the red wool in Susan's yarn box, not knowing that it had been bought for her sweater.

"It's snowing awfully hard," Wanda observed, and she left her chair to stand at the window. "Everything's all covered. Do you think people can get to places?"

"The wind's blowing pretty hard," Susan said, "but we're all right. The clinic's closed today, and you and I have everything we need. Doc says the roads get high drifts, but we'll see. Hurry. Vera wants you to come over and help cut out cookies. Scat! I have surprise things to do."

It continued to snow all day, and when Tim came over around five that afternoon, he told her that the roads were almost impassable.

"Soon as they plow them out, it blows back," he said, closing the cellar door with a thump. "They say this is the worst snow we've had in twenty years or more, and I believe it's longer than that. It's a good night to stay in and look for Santa. Our kids are getting scared he won't be able to get here. I told them it's a good thing he's got his reindeer."

"Tim, have you noticed anything unusual about Wanda?"

"Now's you mention it, I have. She's kind of quiet and more worried about the roads than the little kids. What's gotten into her, do you think?"

"I don't know. She's been worried about whether it would snow for over a week. Today she's so quiet. I've tried asking her, but I haven't been able to get anything out of her."

"There's no telling what kids are thinking about. Maybe part of her does believe in Santa Claus, and it's worrying her that he won't come, or maybe she just doesn't like snow."

"Maybe," Susan said, just as the doorbell rang.

"Who can that be?" Tim said. "Can't anybody get over the roads? Want me to go and see?"

"No, that's all right." If she told the truth, she'd have to admit that she felt restless and shut in.

"Why don't I just peep out?" She heard him walk over to the one-way glass in the front door. "You won't believe it, doctor, but it's Mr. Ward." Tim opened the door, pushing hard against the wind.

"Ho, ho, ho!" Dave said, forcing the heavy door shut against the wind and snow.

"Where's your sleigh?" Tim said. "Here, give me the things, and get out of that coat. He really does look like Santa, doctor. You should see how he's bundled up."

"Hello, Susan. I'm taking you up on your invitation to dinner, but I brought a contribution. Am I welcome?"

"Of course." What else could she say with Tim standing there, probably grinning like the Cheshire Cat? Resentment rose in her. To be fair, though, Dave had no way of knowing that she wouldn't be alone.

"Hang your things in the lavatory over there, and come on up," she told him.

"We'll ride herd on Wanda awhile longer," Tim said. "You go on doctor, and get your supper fixed. Kids just get under your feet like a cat in the kitchen, especially on Christmas Eve. See you."

"How did you get here?" she asked, curious in spite of her annoyance with him.

"I told you I was coming," he said as they started up the stairs. "I did mean to call and ask if it was all right, but the reason I couldn't is quite a story.

"I plan to run a feature on the folklore of the New Year. I was supposed to interview old Mr. Hudson up in Jennings' Gap. Well, to make a long story short, I was there when it started to snow last night. He insisted that I spend the night, and the car's still there."

"How did you get here?"

"The oldest method in the world--I walked."

"All the way in the snow? You're kidding!"

"Well, sort of. He lent me a pair of snowshoes, and that is the truth. It was fun. I had already packed your Christmas things in the car, so all I had to do was load them in the backpack that was still there from last fall, and here I am. Here, here's my-- well, Mr. Hudson's-- contribution to the Christmas Eve feast."

Susan smelled it then, the unmistakable odor of the local country ham.

"He has a liberal hand with the slicing", Dave said as he placed the package of ham slices in her hand.

"There's enough there for an army. He just kept on, especially when he knew where I was going."

"I don't believe any of this. Yes, I do, but to think that this time last year I was tucked in safe and sound in Washington."

"Am I welcome, Sue?" His voice had lost its light, bantering tone.

"Of course you are. Oh, Dave, I've missed you."

And she found herself held close to him, and both of them were laughing and crying at the same time.

"I tried to tell myself that it wasn't worth risking the hurt, but I just couldn't," he whispered. "I'd have risked more than that storm to get here. It's funny, but it seemed so important to be with you tonight. I can't explain it. It was almost a compulsion."

"Probably Mr. Hudson's bed was hard," she said, drying her eyes. "Incidentally, what were you doing still there when the storm started?"

"If you know Mr. Hudson, you shouldn't have to ask. The poor old guy lives alone way out there, and when he gets an audience, he holds on to it."

"It's a wonder you got away tonight." She had started to rummage around for the ingredients for an omelet to go with the ham.

"Oh, he's a romantic. He loved the idea of my snowshoeing to spend Christmas Eve with you."

Together they fixed supper, and it seemed to Susan that they had been working together all her life. She knew she shouldn't be doing this. She would only hurt him, but just for that night, that moment, they were happy.

Wanda was unusually quiet all through dinner, and when Susan told her it was time to go to bed, she went without a word.

"What's wrong with Miss Sunshine?" Dave asked when they had finished the dishes and gone into the living room.

"I don't know," Susan said, starting the stereo. Percy Faith's rendition of "White Christmas" seemed to fill the room. "She's been that way all day."

"She's not sick, is she?"

"I don't think so. I suppose she could be coming down with a cold, or maybe she misses her mother and father. No matter what, they are her parents."

"I guess we've all forgotten that. Maybe she's homesick."

At that moment, "White Christmas" ground to a whining stop.

"The power's off," Dave said. "All the lights went out too. I'm not surprised. This is a wet, heavy snow. That's a lot of weight on the lines. Got any candles?"

In answer, she handed him the two brass holders from the mantel.

"Good thing it's Christmas," she said, holding out a box of kitchen matches, "or I might not have had any. Those holders were empty until I bought the candles for Christmas."

"Is that fireplace just for looks?" he asked. The acrid smell of wax told her that the candles were lit.

"Oh, it's for real. Doc had the chimney checked and cleaned right after I moved. We've had several fires."

"Good, at least we won't freeze, although I imagine that monster in the cellar will put out heat for a while until it eats all its coal. It's fed by an electric stoker, isn't it?"

"Yes, but there's a generator if we really need it. Maybe we'll have current before too long, though."

"Don't count on it. It looks like another world out there--everything's covered with snow. With that wind blowing, you wouldn't believe how deep some of those drifts are."

"Dr. Susan," Wanda called, "my light won't come on."

"It's all right. The power's off, that's all. Would you like me to bring you a flashlight? There are several downstairs."

"No, thank you. I'm not afraid of the dark. I just wondered what time it is."

Susan touched the hands of her watch. "It's almost ten o'clock. Are you warm enough, honey?"

"Yes, thank you, but I have another blanket if I get cold."

"All right. Do you want anything?" "No, thank you. Dr. Susan, do you think any cars can get here tonight?"

"I don't think so. Why?"

"Oh, I just wondered. Good night." "Good night, Wanda. We're right here if you want anything. Just call, okay?" Dave told the child.

"Everything sounds funny," Susan said. "I mean nothing's making a sound, either inside or out."

He pulled her closer to him on the sofa. "On a night like this, you can imagine what it must have been like two hundred years ago. They must have used this very fireplace and candles just like these.

"Think of all the people who were born and who died here. An old house like this makes you feel just how small and unimportant we really are, doesn't it?"

"We are small, I guess, in the whole scheme of things. Yet, how important each of us is to the whole."

"Did you hear something?" She raised her head from his shoulder to listen.

"It's probably the wind. These walls are so thick that you can hardly hear it, but it's really blowing."

"I guess, but it sounded like someone calling."

"Probably that tomcat of Vera's," he said as he pulled her close again. "That beast sounds exactly like a baby crying."

"No, this sounded like a man's voice. I'm probably too taken up with the past. Now I'm hearing things."

"Are you getting cold?" he asked. "Why don't I touch a match to those logs on the hearth before it gets really cold in here?"

"Sounds good to me," she said.

"I think we need a little more kindling," he said. "Is there any around?"

"I think there's some in the cellar. I'll come down too and get a flashlight for you. It'll be easier to manage than one of the candles."

"Give me your hand," he said, "and you can guide me down to the flashlight. You're right, I don't like carrying a candle any more than I have to."

"You mean you trust me," she said, offering him her arm.

They had just reached the bottom of the stairs when they heard it--a man's voice calling, they couldn't tell what.

"There," she said. "That's what I heard before, only now it's closer."

"Get me that flashlight, and I'll have a look. Maybe Tim came out without a good light. It's possible for a person to get lost out there the way that stuff's blowing."

It was then that someone pounded on the front door. "I'll go if you don't mind," he said, taking the flashlight from her.

"The honor's yours. It's hard to imagine anyone or anything alive out in that."

She was standing well back, but it seemed to Susan that the wind would blow her over as the door was opened. It came howling in with such force that she felt helpless in the assault of noise. Then she was back to normal as the heavy door slammed, and all was quiet again.

Then she heard slippered feet coming down the stairs, and Wanda's happy voice saying, "You came! Oh, Jenny, you did come, just like you said you would! You came for Christmas."

"Here we are, honey," a man's voice said, "but we thought we wouldn't make it. You run back up before you get cold. Jenny's tired. Let her rest for a while.

"She needs help, quick," the same voice said in an undertone. "I don't want to scare Wanda. Can you get her back upstairs, please?"

Susan could hear the fatigue and something like desperation in the voice, and without questions, she reacted.

"Do what he asks, please, Wanda. It's all right, but I need you to get some blankets and things together for me. Here, take this flashlight. You know where the linens are kept. Now go, please. You're the only one who can right now. You know where things are."

"But Dr. Susan--"

Susan felt like a traitor when she said the one thing she knew was guaranteed to move the trusting little girl: "Go on now. I need you to be my eyes."

Without another word, Wanda turned, and Susan could hear the little slippers hurrying along the upper hall toward the linen closet.

# Chapter Fifteen

"**S**usan, this is Buddy Ross, and Wanda's sister, Jenny," Dave said.

"I'd figured that out from Wanda's joy. Come on, let's not stand here. You must be almost frozen."

"Jenny and I are married, and she's going to have a baby soon," Buddy said, his words coming out in a rush.

"That's even more reason for us not to stand here in the front hall."

Susan's professional ear told her that he was almost hysterical.

"Dave, the generator's out back. Would you mind seeing about it? Or better still, let's get Tim. He knows all about the beast, I can call him from here at the reception desk."

But when she lifted the receiver, she found that the line was dead.

"The storm must have taken out the telephones along with the electricity," she said, replacing the receiver.

"I'm not surprised," Dave said. "I'll go over and get him. I think he can do a better job with the generator than I can."

"Good. Let's go and sit down. The first examining room's large and has enough chairs, I think. When is your baby due, Jenny?"

"Not for almost another month, but I've been having pains ever since this afternoon."

Susan caught the fear in Jenny's voice, and she put an arm around her.

"It's all right. The first one never seems to do quite what we expect. Let's take off your coat and things."

That's all we need, she thought, as she helped Jenny's cold, numb fingers with the snaps on her coat, a preemie in the middle of a blizzard!

"How did you get here?" she asked, throwing the coat across a chair.

"I have four-wheel drive," Buddy said, "and we did okay until after we turned off the state road. Then we didn't do so well. We got stuck in a drift. We walked the rest of the way. If I hadn't known the area so well, we'd have been completely lost. I centered in on that big pine at the entrance to your drive and kept my eyes on it. It's so tall I was able to keep track of it."

"Was Wanda looking for you to come tonight?" "Yes," Jenny said. "I've been writing to her ever since we left. She knows about the baby, and I told her we'd be home for Christmas. It meant so much to her, and we thought we'd have time--before the baby, I mean. I want my baby to be born here."

Children of the mountain, following the most primitive instinct of man or animal, returning to the place of their birth for the birth of their own children. Susan felt tears come to her eyes. Although she knew they were only a few years younger than she was, she had such a protective feeling toward them.

"I'd say you got here in good time," she told them. "Jenny, I'm not practicing medicine anymore, of course, but if you trust me, I'll have a look. I think we need to know how much time we have."

"Of course I don't mind, Susan. Wanda thinks you can move the world. Why shouldn't I trust you?"

Susan could think of a lot of reasons, but she kept them to herself.

"All right, then. We'll chase Buddy to the kitchen at the back of the hall to make some coffee. It's a gas stove, thank goodness. I think you'll find whatever you need."

"Sure, don't worry about that, but why don't I get Wanda to help? I hear her coming."

"Great," Susan said, "but let her come and give Jenny a hug. She's been watching and praying for you to come all day."

"You didn't say what you wanted, Dr. Susan, but I brought some sheets and blankets. Is that all right?"

"Perfect. You come and kiss Jenny, and then go and help Buddy make coffee. You know where Miss Ellen puts things when she washes them before the office closes."

"Oh, Jenny, I'm so glad to see you!" Wanda said, and Susan could hear tears in her voice. "I was so scared that you wouldn't come, and you and Buddy were all I wanted for Christmas."

"We'll do better than that." Susan could hear the fatigue in Jenny's voice. "We brought presents, and the baby's going to be a Christmas baby."

"Oh, Jenny, really? I know all about babies, Dr. Susan. It's sort of like Penelope, only she has a lot of babies all at the same time."

Susan experienced the giggly feeling she had every time Wanda mentioned Penelope the pig, but she managed to control it.

"Good, I'm glad to know that. You know, then, how important it is for you to do just as I ask you. And now will you go and help Buddy, please?"

"I certainly will," she said in her most grown-up way and went skipping down the hall calling, "I'm coming, Buddy."

"We still have some time," Susan said, as she dropped the glove she'd been using into the trash pail. "I want you to relax as much as possible, and try not to worry."

"I'm not worried, now that we're here. It was the cold and the snow that worried me. I know I'm in good hands," Jenny told her.

"I'll go and see how the coffee's coming along. Just lie there. I'll be back in a minute."

"Is everything all right?" Buddy asked when Susan pushed through the swinging door into the room that had once been the butler's pantry and now served as the kitchen for coffee and snacks.

"Wanda honey, would you mind going upstairs and putting the screen in front of the fireplace? We had started to make a fire, and I can't remember whether we had actually put a match to it or not. Then get some of the ham left from supper, and why don't you put some rolls in the oven in my kitchen?"

"I'll fix a good supper--you can count on me."

"I know you will," Susan said, hugging her. "Dr. Susan, are you mad at me?"

"Why should I be?"

"Because I didn't tell you they were coming. It was supposed to be a secret. I'm sorry."

"There's nothing to be sorry about. You have a right to your secrets, the same as anyone else. I am curious, though. How did you manage to keep it a secret? Didn't anybody see the letters?"

"No. When I was at home, I always got the mail, and Mama couldn't read very well. Then here at the clinic, I picked up the mail for Miss Ellen every day."

Susan gave her another hug. "Go get the things ready. Take the big flashlight on the reception desk, and don't hurry too much."

"Oh, I won't. I'll be careful."

"Has Jenny been getting regular medical attention?" she asked as soon as the door had shut behind Wanda.

"Yes. Is something wrong?" Buddy asked.

"The baby seems to be turned wrong. It isn't life-threatening, especially if it's handled right. I didn't mention it to her. I wanted to talk to you first."

"The doctor at the clinic where she'd been going--actually, it was a different doctor each time--said that the delivery might be a hard one, but that it wasn't anything to worry about. That was the last time she went, a few days ago."

"Normally, of course, it wouldn't be anything to worry about, but tonight is hardly normal. She'll need more care than would be normal too. Oh, I hate even thinking about this, but I can't give it to her."

"But you're a doctor. I don't care if you can't see with your eyes, you're still a doctor."

"You don't understand. I can't, I just can't."

"You can't what?" She hadn't heard the door open, and when Dave spoke, she jumped.

Quickly, she told him about the situation. "You'll have to get Doc somehow," she finished.

"No way, Sue," he said. "You remember, Doc was going to visit his sister in South Carolina. They left yesterday."

"Sorry, I had forgotten. Then get Bill."

"Normally, that wouldn't be a problem, but there's no way we can get there. Bill's off on a side road worse than this one, and you can't even tell where this road is. It's as though there's no road there. Buddy, it's a miracle you got here."

"You've got to try." Susan could feel the panic rising in her. "We can't just stand here saying that this storm's going to defeat us. We're talking about two lives. Can't you understand that?"

He took her hands. "If I thought there was a chance, I'd start out now on my snowshoes, but it's too far, you know that. Even if I got there and even if Bill got back, it would be too late."

"We have to do something."

"Yes, we do. But you're the one who can do it. Susan, you're a doctor. You can do it. I know you can, believe me."

"I'm a doctor who can't see. Don't you know I would if I could? But I can't! I can't take the risk. Oh, don't you know how much I want to do it?"

"You can do it," he said, and the words were a gentle whisper. "The knowledge is there, Susan, in your fingertips, in your brain, and in your very spirit. You had it when you could see, and you still have it."

"But--"

"He's right, Susan," Buddy said. "Wanda wrote and told us that you helped her. You can do this, I know you can. God wouldn't have brought us home for anything bad to happen. Please, you're all we have."

"This isn't the same. All I did for Wanda was to administer an already-measured dose of medication. This is different."

"Sue, if you don't face this--no matter what the outcome is--you'll always wonder. Someday you'll hate yourself for not trying, and soon after that, you'll start to hate us for witnessing your fear. Don't you see, darling, you must do this--not only for Jenny and the baby but for yourself, for us."

She stood there, remembering another time, another place when she had remembered her sworn duty to preserve life. Could she turn away from it now? She knew Dave was right. No matter how she shrank from it, she would hate herself if she didn't at least try.

"Suppose I fail. They could both die."

"They'll both die if you don't try," Buddy said.

"All right, all right, I'll try. Dave, go get Vera. I'll have to have help. I just hope she doesn't panic."

"I've taken the class," Buddy said. "I had planned to be there in the delivery room. Do you think I'd be any help?"

She thought for a minute and then said, "Yes.

Come on, and we'll get things ready. But before that, will you please tell me why all the secrecy about coming back."

"Do you know why we left?"

"Yes. I'll have to say I thought it was pretty silly, but I know."

"We didn't want Mama and Dad to know we were coming. It was dumb, I guess, but we knew there'd be a big fuss about it. We figured that if we just showed up for Christmas, they'd give in, especially with the baby on the way. How were we to know we'd find ourselves in the middle of a blizzard?"

"Now you'll have not just a baby on the way, but a real, live baby," Susan said, and with the words, she had made her commitment, not only to deliver the baby but to save it too.

At first, Susan had been sure that her commitment was in vain, but as she used the old movements, the old skill came back. Sometimes for long periods, she didn't even think about not being able to see as her fingers, made sensitive by months of use in partial substitution for her sight, moved almost on their own.

Vera and Buddy proved to be good helpers, and Jenny herself spurred her on with her unfailing confidence in her and faith in God.

"It's a girl--I just know it," Jenny said once after an especially hard pain. "I'm going to name it for Mama Ross and you, Susan. How does Susan Ann grab you? Ann is Mama Ross's middle name."

"It's beautiful," Susan said, remembering the other Anne who had helped to make this night possible for her. Oh, dear God, please, please let it be all right. "What, I wonder, though, will you do if it's a boy?"

"Oh, it won't be. We want the first one to be a girl, and I just know it will be, just as I know it's going to be all right. Buddy, do you think you can get Mama Ross over to see the baby when she's born?"

"Just as soon as it's light, Dave's going over on his snowshoes," Buddy said. "I don't know how she'll get back, but Dad will figure something out. Don't worry."

"Do you think it'll be all right, with them, I mean?"

"I think they were sorry a long time ago," Susan said. "Only, they didn't know just how to say they'd been silly, not to mention that they didn't know how to find you. I never saw a grandma and grandpa yet who didn't forget everything else in the world when brought face-to-face with the first grandchild. This time, you know, it'll be sort of a double grandchild."

"We didn't handle the whole thing too well, did we?" Buddy said. "I have a temper, and so does Dad. I think Mama and Jenny just got dragged along. Dad had a sister, his oldest sister, who married an adopted brother. There was probably something wrong with him, emotionally, I mean, because it never worked, and finally, he ended up killing her and then himself. They were living in Arkansas, and people around here don't know anything about it. I think Dad was somehow getting the two things mixed up in the part of his mind that fears unreasonable things. He kept saying it was like brother and sister, but it was never like that for us, Susan."

"I'm sure it wasn't, but you're right that all of us mix things up in our minds."

And she was remembering Eric's possessiveness and his fear of public opinion. How could she have thought Dave would be like that? It wasn't a bit hard, her mind told her.

# Chapter Sixteen

I t was just at dawn, that hour when life so often leaves the body, that the new life made its entrance. As always, Susan thrilled to the miracle of the tiny being who--in part because of her-- had made the perilous journey into the world. She knew that probably this would be the last time she would feel that thrill, but the knowledge didn't make her feel sad. Deep inside herself, she knew that she, too, had made her way on a perilous journey toward a new life.

"Jenny Ross," she said, "meet Susan Ann. She's so tiny, but she's fine. And she's so beautiful! I can't see her, but, oh, Jenny, she's so beautiful."

"She's little, all right," Vera said, "but there's nothing wrong with the way she can cry. Want me to take her, Dr. Susan? I've got a nice little basket fixed with blankets and hot water bottles, just the way you said."

"That's great, Vera. Thank you and Buddy for all your help. I couldn't possibly have done it without you."

And suddenly, Buddy was hugging her. She felt the tears of relief on his cheeks, mingling with her own.

"Thank you, Susan," he said. "We'll never forget you, never."

"You don't need to thank me," she told him. "You don't know how much I have to thank you for. Let's let Jenny rest--she deserves it. I think we could use some coffee."

With the coming of dawn, the storm seemed to blow itself out. The wind, which had threatened the sturdy old pines, died to what might almost be called a breeze. The snowflakes, which had fallen so thick and fast, began to fall slowly, the last feathers from a giant pillow; then they stopped altogether.

By nine o'clock, a brilliant sun turned the whole world into one big, dazzling Christmas card.

The power company had restored service a little after seven, and around nine-thirty, the phone rang.

"It was Bill," Susan told Dave when she came back to the dining alcove. "He called to see if Wanda and I were all right. I think he's probably still wondering if I celebrated well but unwisely last night. He could hardly believe all the things I told him."

Dave laughed and pushed a full mug of coffee under her hand. "I'll have to admit that sometimes I can't believe it either."

"Bill got in touch with the county about a snowplow for our road even before he called me. Jenny and Susan Ann are doing fine, but I'd like to get Susan Ann into an incubator for a couple of days. Bill's arranging for the ambulance from the Rescue Squad to pick them up. He'll meet them at the hospital."

"Will you be going with them?"

"No way. Bill's taking over. "I have seen my duty and I have done it," as they say, but I'm more than glad to hand them over to him."

"I'm awfully proud of you, you know," he said, taking her hand across the coffee mugs.

"I suppose that if I'm honest, I'll have to say that I'm proud of myself too. But you'll never know how scared I was."

"No, I'm sure I won't, but I can imagine. I knew you'd come through, though."

"I almost forgot to ask. How did you get along with the Rosses? Until today I really never knew just how much care a tiny baby takes. I just delivered them and turned them over to someone else. I've hardly had a minute all morning."

"They acted just the way we'd thought they would. I didn't even mention the trouble. I just told them that Buddy and Jenny were married, and had come to surprise them and Wanda for Christmas. I also mentioned that they had a granddaughter."

"What did they do then?" Susan was enjoying this.

"They acted predictably: Sarah cried, and Ezra made growling noises. They wanted to start right over on foot, but I finally persuaded them to wait. I figured the plow would be along pretty soon."

"Can you imagine Wanda keeping all that to herself? At her age, I'd have blabbed it all over the place. What do you suppose Social Services will do about a home for her?"

"I'm sure Buddy and Jenny would love to have her. Buddy is studying agriculture on a scholarship, and he hopes to teach around here someplace. I expect his folks will help."

"If Buddy and Jenny can't take Wanda, maybe the Rosses will take her," Susan said. "I think they would have taken her to live with them a long time ago if her mother hadn't been opposed. It seems pretty likely, though, that we'll never see her mother again. Do you think her father would agree to it?"

"I think he'd be glad, but the Rosses aren't as young as they used to be."

Susan remembered her own quiet childhood. No, she didn't want that for Wanda, who was so bright, so full of life. No, that wouldn't be such a good idea.

In the distance, she could hear the rumble of the snowplow, accompanied by the moan of the ambulance, which had slowed its pace to that of the plow.

Again, she was back in another place, listening to the moan of another ambulance as it came to a stop. It seemed a lifetime since she had looked for the last time at the day slowly giving way to the night. She had come a long way, she knew --a long, long way in so many respects.

"I need to go down and be sure that Jenny and Susan Ann are ready," she said, pushing back her chair.

"I'll wait for you unless there's something I can do to help."

"No, not a thing, but thanks."

As Susan came back up the stairs almost an hour later, she wondered if Dave would still be waiting. She had misjudged just how long it would take for the road to be plowed. Part of her had been glad to have the extra time. She knew that Dave might be about to ask something of her that, in spite of her newfound confidence, she might not be ready to give.

"Everything all right?" he asked as she came into the living room.

"Fine. Jack Martin was with the ambulance, and he knows his stuff, but I think Jenny was glad to have me there. I guess I'd better get the breakfast dishes cleaned up." She started toward the kitchen.

"You can't put it off forever, Sue. Come and sit down. I cleaned up in the kitchen ages ago, and don't tell me you have to do something else, because I'm not going to accept it."

"All right," she said, and she sat beside him on the sofa.

"Merry Christmas," he said softly, placing a small package in her hand.

"Christmas! My goodness, I forgot. Poor little Wanda! Dave, I'm sorry, but I have to give her presents. She's with Vera's children, and she must be feeling awful, watching them open their things."

"She's all right. Sit down. I took her packages over when you left. I think I got everything. I took what was under the tree. Was that all?"

"Yes, but I wanted this Christmas to be so special for her!"

"It is. She was having a ball with Vera's little niece when I left. Do you think anything could be more special for her than to have Buddy and Jenny back, not to mention the baby? If I know kids, she and the other little girls are whispering about babies. We'll have some time to spend with her later."

"I'm sure you're right, but--" "Susan, don't run away. I'll walk out of your life if you want me to, but please open your present first, and let's at least talk about things."

"I'm sorry. I think I'm still uptight from last night. Of course, I don't want you to go. Your present is under the tree."

"Okay, but you first."

She removed the satin ribbon and then the heavy embossed paper. How like Dave to select a paper that was beautiful to the touch!

"May I?" he asked. And, without waiting for her answer, he took the box.

"I think it'll fit," he said, and he slipped a ring on her finger.

"Dave, I--"

"You don't have to keep it, but I hope you will. It's a diamond cluster. I closed my eyes and looked at every ring on the tray. I wanted to see them the way you would. I think this one is the prettiest."

"Oh, Dave, it is beautiful! But ... suppose I can't give to you the way I should?"

"May I ask you something?"

"Of course." She fingered the pattern of diamonds.

"Do you love me? Take your time and think about it, because your love is the only thing you'd have to give. You're a person, Sue. I'd never ask for anything that would diminish that person in the slightest, because I love you as a person, as a woman."

"But who am I, really?" she asked. "I'm not sure that I know."

"Yes, you do. You faced yourself last night, and whether you know it or not, you conquered something in yourself when you faced and conquered death."

They sat close together, not touching, not speaking. Finally, she spoke.

"You're right. Only, I was afraid to admit it. That new life I helped to bring into the world is symbolic of my new self. I didn't want to let go of the old any more than Susan Ann wanted to give up her nice, warm resting place. As long as I stayed in my little nest inside myself, without depending on anyone or allowing anyone to depend on me, I thought nothing could hurt me."

"But you started to come out of your safe little nest when you took Wanda to stay with you. Social Services could have found a home for her, you know that. You wanted, needed her as much for your good as for hers."

She nodded. "You're right. I think--no, I know--I'll miss her when she goes."

"She doesn't have to go. She could live with us. Susan, I love you, and I want you to marry me--not for Wanda, not even for you, but for myself. I want us to spend our lives together the way my parents did, the way Sarah and Ezra are doing."

He stood up and pulled her with him. "Now," he said, "I've said it. It's up to you. If you really want me to, I'll take back my ring and get out of your life, but I'll never feel quite the same.

There will always be an empty place in my life and in my heart, which only you and your love can fill."

For an answer, she held out her arms, reaching to him. He came into them, and they stood together in an embrace that joined them as one--separate bodies, separate minds, but one spirit, one heart, united forever by love. She had found her place, her home at last.

# THE END

CPSIA information can be obtained
at www.ICGtesting.com
Printed in the USA
BVHW040946220720
584331BV00006B/35